PUSHCARTS AND DREAMERS

PUSHCARTS AND DREAMERS

*Stories of
Jewish life in America*

by

SHOLEM ASCH
BORUCH GLASMAN
LEON KOBRIN
ZALMAN LIBIN
MOISHE NADIR
JOSEPH OPATOSHU
CHAVER PAVER
ISAAC RABOI
ABRAHAM REISIN
JONAH ROSENFELD

*Edited, Translated and
with an Introduction by*

MAX ROSENFELD

SOUTH BRUNSWICK
NEW YORK ● LONDON

THOMAS YOSELOFF

*Library of Congress
Catalog Card Number: 67-22185*

SBN
498-06984-2

Printed in the United States of America

*Dedicated to the
memory of*
FRED H. GREENBERG,
*good friend,
whose loving care
and direction are
on every page of
this book*

Illustrations / EVERETT H. SOLOVITZ
Initials / LEON BESKRONE
Portrait Sketches / EDWARD MOSKOW
Typography / FRED H. GREENBERG

Contents

Acknowledgements

I wish to express my deep appreciation to Mrs. Elsie Levitan and Mr. Itche Goldberg for their editorial help. This book is a better one for it.

I wish also to thank the following, who generously gave their time and talents to the artistic and technical tasks which go into the making of a book: Fred Greenberg, Max Millman, Everett Solovitz, Edward Moskow, Leon Beskrone, Florence Olivenbaum, Bess Katz, Morris Weiss. They have helped to make this book a truly collective achievement of the Sholom Aleichem Club itself. My special thanks to Rose Rosenfeld, who in addition to technical assistance, provided the right word of wifely encouragement.

To Mrs. Bea Katz, Mr. Sol Rotenberg and Mr. Leon Tissian, my gratitude for having the vision and practical confidence that such a project could be brought to fruition..

M. R.

Introduction

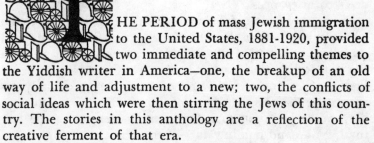HE PERIOD of mass Jewish immigration to the United States, 1881-1920, provided two immediate and compelling themes to the Yiddish writer in America—one, the breakup of an old way of life and adjustment to a new; two, the conflicts of social ideas which were then stirring the Jews of this country. The stories in this anthology are a reflection of the creative ferment of that era.

A brief look at a few figures will indicate the tremendous changes that took place during those years in the Jewish population of the United States.

At the beginning of 1881 there were about 300,000 Jews here, most of whom—though not all—had originated from non-Yiddish-speaking Jewish communities in Central and Western Europe. During the next ten years the first significant wave of Yiddish-speaking Jews arrived in this country, and then, between 1890 and 1920, more than 2,000,000 Jews fled to America from Russia, Poland, Roumania and Austria-Hungary. "A whole people moved across the ocean on boats," wrote Sholem Asch.

It is from these East European, Yiddish-speaking immigrants that at least 85 percent of today's American Jews are descended.

Like all the other immigrants—and the Jews were only a small percentage of all the immigrants—the Jews came to America in search of freedom, freedom from oppression and freedom to earn their living in peace. The Jews in Eastern Europe, in addition, had been singled out for national persecution in a part of the world where political and economic backwardness were rampant. Jews were restricted as to where they could live, what occupations and professions they could follow, what education they could receive. They had no political rights and certainly no channels for a "redress of grievances."

Yet most of them came from towns and townlets (*shtetlech*) where their families had lived for generations. They had grown up in a way of life shaped by cultural isolation from the non-Jewish world around them and by a pattern of religious observance which affected every aspect of daily existence. Jewishness was a way of living into which you were born and which you took for granted—along with the cultural, group and family values of the tradition.

More frightful and alarming than the political and economic deprivation were the pogroms, which ravaged hundreds of Jewish communities in southern Russia. These anti-Semitic riots, which at first were a means of diverting the discontent of the Russian people, later became part of the terror let loose by the government itself against the movement to overthrow the autocracy. Many Jews—mostly young men and women—were direct or indirect participants in the democratic upsurge against Czarist tyranny, and they brought with them to America their fervent enthusiasm for a better social order.

All the immigrants set out for the New World full of hope that life would be better. And life here *was* better, freer. But it was also strange and unfamiliar. And the word "better" must be qualified.

The physical conditions into which most of the *first* Jewish immigrants were thrown were unspeakable—not only by today's standards, but by the standards of the victims themselves. They came here penniless and they were forced to work for a pittance. Those who had no trade took to peddling—which was not exactly an easy or lucrative livelihood. Or they sorted rags. Or they made cigars. Some few became metal workers. Those who managed to learn to ply a needle or run a Singer sewing machine worked in dark, crowded, gloomy sweatshops 15 to 18 hours a day and ate and slept in dark, crowded, gloomy tenements. (The first arrivals here in the early 1880s were generally not the skilled artisans or experienced factory workers. Later, a considerable number of the Jewish immigrants came from some of the larger cities of Russia, where they had already worked in such industries as clothing, textile and tobacco. Some had been educated in Russian schools and could speak and read Russian fluently.)

But that is not the whole story. The bright side of the story is the battle the Jewish immigrants waged here to put an end to their inhuman conditions. They did it individually and they did it collectively. They waged the good fight instinctively and they waged it advisedly—following the teachings of the social and political movements which at that time were offering solutions to society's ills. And of these solutions there was a considerable variety—socialism practical and socialism utopian, anarchism philosophical and anarchism of the deed, trade unionism, back-to-the-soilism, political Zionism, cultural Zionism, territorialism—and each movement had its teachers, its publications, its lectures, its meetings, and its passionate conviction that whatever it was that needed doing must be done *now*.

The initiative and the drive in these movements came from the radical students and intellectuals imbued with the democratic and socialist ideals then agitating the thinking youth of a good part of the world. Energetic, determined, self-sacrificing, they regarded it as their social duty to educate the Jewish working-people—of which many of them became a part—and to help in establishing the economic and political organizations which would solve their problems.

The Jewish labor movement, which grew out of this activity, was *not* an isolated enclave in a hostile American world. This was a time of social ferment, of new, revolutionary ideas among large groups of native Americans and immigrants of other nationalities. The working people of the United States were astir. Agitation for the eight-hour day was widespread. This was the formative period of the mass labor movement which was later to play such an important part in American life. ("We sought the advice of leaders of other unions, of the progressive German workers, who at that time were close to us. They then had large, strong unions in New York and other cities, and we, the founders and leaders of the Jewish unions, used to learn from them. . . . The first thing we learned from them was that in order to create a labor movement and organize unions we must first have our own newspaper.")[1]

---

1. The Jewish Unions in America, Bernard Weinstein, New York, 1929.

The Yiddish writers represented in this anthology were, for the most part, closely aligned with the cultural and political movements which were then having such a deep-going effect upon the Yiddish reader—expanding his horizon and encouraging common action with his fellows to improve his everyday life.

And his life was hard. Hard, but not bleak. Hard, but not humorless, not dull, not unthinking, not static. On the contrary, no period in American Jewish history was or has been as ideologically stormy as that one. How could it have been bleak when the underlying idea of all the various social movements—no matter how far apart on "tactics"—was an optimistic one: *Man could improve his condition.* The enemy of progress was powerful and all-pervasive and there was no agreement or clearly-defined plan of action on how he would be overcome, but one thing was certain—Man could improve his own condition, by his own efforts, through organization and mass activism.

It should be no mystery, therefore, that for at least two generations of American Jews it was an unquestioned and self-evident truth of life that trade unions are a blessing to mankind.

Leon Kobrin, in his autobiography, quotes a Jewish intellectual reminiscing about those years. "It was a wonderful time! How beautifully people lived, how beautifully they believed, those non-believers! . . . People debated fervently and argued heatedly with each other—and mostly it was not out of envy or hatred, but out of love for humanity and devotion to an ideal. . . . Most of them were half-educated? Also true. But they were all poets with beautiful worlds in their imaginations, with tremendous creative energy in their blood and with a fanatically-stubborn faith. . . . All our labor organizations, our newspapers, our better theater, our literature—whatever Jewish culture we possess here, in its best form—they were the ones who built it."[2]

An early historian of that period, examining the connection between Jewish politics and Jewish culture, summed it up this way: "The history of Yiddish literature is to a certain degree the history of the cultural growth of the Jewish workingman. They grew up together like twins. They influenced each other equally. The Jewish worker became progressive because he grew up on a progressive Yiddish literature; Yiddish literature had to be progressive because it was the literature of the awakening workingman. And therefore, in fact, everything that is talented in Yiddish is more or less progressive."[3]

Half a century later the sociologist C. Bezalel Sherman is able to say categorically of this productive era of American Jewish experience: "An extensive Jewish culture developed parallel with the rise of the Jewish labor movement and in large measure as a result of it. A Yiddish literature of great scope was created, *the most important non-English literature ever to arise in the United States.*" [4]

And the American critic Irving Howe, in an essay written for the Jewish Museum exhibition "The Lower East Side," defining the *Yiddishkeit* of that milieu, says: ". . . It meant cultural intensity, indeed, cultural ferocity; it placed commitment before manners, vitality before gentility. . . . And it served as a common norm or reference by means of which a beleaguered community would try to regulate its terms of existence."[5]

It would be a mistake, however, to conclude from all this

2. Leon Kobrin, *My Fifty Years in America*, Buenos Aires, 1955. The speaker was Dr. Charles Spivak, founder of the Denver Sanatorium.
3. S. K. Snefal, *Der Arbeiter Ring*, 1910.
4. *The Jew Within American Society*, Detroit, 1965. (My emphasis.)
5. *The Lower East Side: Portal to American Life*, The Jewish Museum, New York, 1966.

that the literature created under these circumstances was purely "didactic" or that, in the Yiddish phrase, it was motivated solely by *tachlis*, by immediate practical purpose. The Yiddish works of this period—of which the stories in this book are a sampling—were created with the same purpose for which any work of art is created—to catch a moment of experience and illuminate it, to make life more comprehensible to its participants, not least of all to the artist himself.

But that this literature was meant to be a source of spiritual strength to the reader is also quite true. Whether designed that way or no, it served to guide him out of his confused "greenhorn" state, to rid him of his first fears, to make him feel like a *mentsh*. It was also, despite the denials of some of its pioneers, (a point we will discuss later), part of an age-old Jewish culture with a long value-tradition— and that value-tradition made itself felt in the work of all Yiddish writers of any merit.

It is not too difficult, consequently, to indicate some of the more easily-definable ideas which emerge from the stories selected for this book, values which were called up out of an old culture to meet new circumstances, and which therefore appeared in a new form: the dignity of labor, the preciousness of human life, the intrinsic worth of the individual human being, the wickedness of war, the community of interest of the Jewish working people, the common aspirations of all the immigrants—Jew and non-Jew alike, the right to be Jewish, the obligation to be kind to "the stranger within thy gates," the indispensability of a sense of humor. All of this is encompassed by the Yiddish phrase which became well-nigh a litany—*far a shenereh, bessereh velt*—the vision of a better, more beautiful world.

The Jewish immigrant had a real need to learn about himself, especially about himself in relation to his new surroundings, and here, too, his literature came to his aid. Obviously, one of the means to his Americanization was to learn English. But just as important was his need to read Yiddish, so that he would more easily and more quickly comprehend the world into which fate had tossed him. American Yiddish literature thus helped in the Americanization process, as the critic Boruch Rivkin points out, because it reflected the reader, "with his thoughts and feelings, gave him a taste of seeing himself 'written up' . . . which in turn gave him a new interest in literature. It thus fulfilled the elementary function of literature—to transform the reader by making him relive his own experience and the experience of his fellows. . . ."

Despite its linguistic relationship to the old country, Yiddish literature in America had to go through its own beginnings, its own primitive stage, its own search for form, all the first steps any new cultural movement must take. Thus, before 1900, there was also in this country a primitive Yiddish "literature" characterized more by quantity than by quality, appearing mostly in the form of sentimental novels —in pamphlet installments—which were grabbed up as soon as they were printed. The literature of any artistic merit, however, first appeared in the labor and socialist newspapers —a short story or a poem bordered on all sides by news and political articles.

In the beginning, no one gave Yiddish or its literature in America an expected life-span of more than 25 years. It was regarded as a temporary phenomenon, almost as a literature created in spite of itself. The idea that Jews in the United States would ever comprise a distinct group with its own cultural needs existed, if at all, in a rudimentary form. And despite the fact that Yiddish literature was then thriving in Europe—the three "greats," Mendele Mocher Sforim, Sholem Aleichem and Peretz, were at the height of their creativity—

the first Yiddish writers in the United States did not consider themselves part of that literature. They were pioneers here, they said—groundbreakers.

"When I came to America in 1892," wrote Leon Kobrin, "the ARBEITER TSEITUNG was already several years old. Yiddish literature was completely unknown to me then. Mendele and Peretz I knew only from one or two Russian translations which I had read in the *Voskhod*. . . . That one could write stories in the Yiddish language never even occurred to me until I came to America. . . . Let me note that the stories of the old country were easier for me to write than those of American life. Writing about Jewish life in Russia, I constantly had before my eyes a defined, developed, complete type, with a definite world outlook, a heritage of generations and generations; but writing about Jewish life in America I constantly had before my eyes confused souls, unsettled characters, a chaotic life. And to create life and people out of chaos—that was easy only for the Almighty Himself![6]

In a relatively short time, however, this chaotic life began to "simmer down." Between 1900 and 1910 (the peak of the mass immigration) a new audience arose which freed the Yiddish writer, to a great extent, from the grip of the daily newspaper. In New York City alone this audience numbered more than a million people, of whom a substantial segment had some knowledge of Russian and Yiddish literature.

Classes, groups, values, began to sort themselves out. The Jewish entity began to take shape. A group consciousness emerged. Writers began to call upon their Jewish spiritual reserves to help them face contemporary problems. Joseph Opatoshu wrote first about Grand Street in New York, but later about the Polish woods of his youth. Leon Kobrin

---

6. Introduction to Collected Stories, 1910.

wrote first about the East Side sweatshops, but later about the Jewish fishermen he had known as a child. Isaac Raboi wrote about the American prairies, but later about the rich earth of Bessarabia, from which his family had come. Sholem Asch wrote about the Jewish factory-owner and his *lantsleit* (whom he both helped and exploited), but the trilogy "Three Cities" is an epic of Jewish familial clans in the turmoil of revolutionary Europe.

Was this only a nostalgia for the past, for the writer's own personal past? Was it only a natural disposition to work with materials bred in his bones? Or could it not also have been an intuitive striving to carry over Jewish historical values to the new, uncertain, formless, crass, American Jewish present? The immigrants had left a milieu that was intensely Jewish. Religious Jewishness here was either frowned upon ideologically by the radicals and union leaders, or else it was so cheapened and debased by the exigencies of the City and Business that it seemed but an empty and meaningless shell, totally irrelevant to the time and to the needs of the masses of American Jews.

Was this concern for the past—which co-existed with the present in the minds of so many of the Yiddish writers—a means of shoring up the self-image of the American Jews as a people? Rivkin calls it an effort to "transform the old faith-force into a modern moral-force." With so much activity and self-sacrifice expected and required of the Jewish common man, where was he to get the strength for all this? If not from his religion, then the Jewish historical reservoir had to be opened wide.

That this is more than philosophical speculation can be seen from what happened to Yiddish literature itself. It became more than "mere literature." It took on a function over and above that of a normal literature. It became a movement. For many Jews it became a way of life, a substi-

tute for religion and the synagogue; it took the place of a
Jewish land—the term "Yiddishland," in fact, came into use
to express the scope and sphere of Yiddish culture generally.
Yiddishkeit (Jewishness) without Yiddish became an in-
conceivable notion. The culture itself came to serve a definite social purpose, deepening the Jewish will to survive
when the world around it challenged the very right of a
Jewish people to exist.

It was natural, therefore, that after a while, the division
between the American and European Yiddish literatures
became less and less distinct. Often they were the product
of the same writer, even though at various times several
of the younger writers here issued manifestos and credos
dissociating themselves from Yiddish writing in Europe and
denying any mutual influences. In an article written in
1915 Morris Winchevsky, who himself had a hand in both
literatures, describes the effect of I. L. Peretz on the American Yiddish writers in the 1890s.

"While there is nothing of Peretz' influence noticeable in
any of them, there is, however, something else that *is* noticeable: The appearance of Peretz' writing in our arena had
the effect of a 'rich uncle' visiting a poor family. Willingly
or unwillingly, they no longer had the brazenness to go
about unkempt, unwashed, in tatters, inside the same house
with the rich uncle. . . . Among the writers, Peretz was
perhaps more widely read than any other. . . ."

In retrospect, American Yiddish literature takes its place
as a branch of *world* Yiddish literature, which has roots
in various and widely-separated soils. The branches of this
literature influence each other's growth, and the fruits of
the tree are enjoyed far beyond the geographical location of
the roots. And they are roots not only in space, but in time
—in the long history of the Jewish people.

The stories selected for this volume reflect experiences common to many American Jews in the early years of this century, experiences which shaped the attitudes and the self-image of American Jewry. "The liberal tradition of American Jewry" has become a familiar phrase. By politicians it is accepted as a fact of life. Where did it come from, this liberal tradition, how was it nurtured, how deep is it —these are questions that can be answered with the help of American Yiddish literature.

"The Jewish tradition of social justice" is another common phrase—echoing the Prophets. Similar questions can be asked about that concept, too. But if it is to mean anything at all, it is a tradition that every generation of Jews must see anew with its own eyes, in relationship to its own circumstances. The Yiddish writers—who were steeped in this tradition even when they rejected its ritual—wove it into the fabric of their works.

The hero of Sholem Asch's "Union for Shabbos" utters the famous battle-cry of Mattathias, the father of the Maccabees, in his strike-call to his fellow shop-workers. In Irving Howe's essay (referred to previously) there is a quotation from an article written by Abraham Cahan in 1898 describing a visit he made to a *mishna* class of striking vestmakers. One of the Jewish vestmakers expressed himself thus: "Ours is a just cause. It is for the bread of our children we are struggling. . . . Saith the Law of Moses: Thou shalt not withhold anything from thy neighbor nor rob him; there shall not abide with thee the wages of him that is hired, through the night until morning. So it stands in Leviticus. So you see that our bosses who rob us . . . commit a sin. . . . What do we come to America for? To bathe in tears, and to see our wives and our children rot in plenty? Tears and sighs we had in plenty in the old country."

Sholem Asch's story has a whimsical air about it, but the

intent is real enough. Perhaps it is real because of this very touch of whimsy—otherwise it might have been nothing more than a propaganda piece.

The Jewish cigarmaker in Kobrin's "Little Souls" finally reaches the point of rebellion against the degradation of another Jew by an Irish foreman, and calls upon the Jewish solidarity of two other workers for a common defense. That he fails because he waited too long is, alas, only an accurate image of reality, a reflection of the "human nature" of human beings, Jew and non-Jew alike. And the surprise ending only points up the human-ness of the degraded— and the artistic integrity of the writer.

The conflicts that developed inside the Jewish community itself between workers and bosses, between Jewish unions and Jewish employers, were dealt with by almost every one of the Yiddish writers of that period. How could they *not* have done so? From a literary standpoint these struggles contained all the necessary ingredients of drama and excitement. From a social viewpoint they were an embodiment of the ancient and recurring conflicts between master and slave, rich and poor, exploiters and exploited, Kings and Prophets.

In Kobrin's story, "A Common Language," another element makes its appearance—the solidarity of Jew and non-Jew against injustice—even if the perpetrator of the injustice is a Jew.

The immigrant fought to assert his dignity as a human being; his efforts took various forms, but they were all part of the same battle against the humiliation of the individual. Several of the stories are concerned with that in one way or another. In Jonah Rosenfeld's "Vreplamrendn" an educated immigrant invents a most original challenge to his landlady and her superior "American" airs. In Opatoshu's "Family Pride" an unemployed worker defies his cousin's nouveau riche insensitivity. The challenges and the defiances had one purpose—to pull the rug from under people with an insufferable air of self-importance, especially those who used their position to lord it over others.

It may be difficult for young American Jews today to realize that their grandparents, when *they* were young, faced unemployment and hunger in the Golden Land. Bernard Weinstein, describing the effect of the 1893 depression on the Jews of New York, writes; "Jewish working-class families were being thrown out of their homes for not paying the rent. The sidewalks of all the East Side streets were blocked by the furniture of evicted tenants. The only consolation was that this misfortune happened in the hot summer months. Tattered workingmen, and women with babies in their arms, used to run around frantically, looking for any sort of work, or for a dry crust of bread for their children. . . . They were ready to do the hardest kind of work for any price. . . ."

To comprehend this aspect of American Jewish history through the eyes of a young boy huckstering apples, or through the emotions of two young women confronted with the choice of breaking open their dime banks or starving, is a good lesson in humility; or at least in gaining a proper perspective toward those who are, in our current terminology, "deprived."

And the father who wonders why his American son must go to war to capture a Mexican general who is "making a revolution" *in his own country* has a remarkably topical ring.

These values are characteristic of Yiddish literature as a whole. In that respect, American Yiddish literature was following in the path of its sister literature in Europe. Without a background of American Yiddish literature, contemporary writing about American Jews is disconnected from a vital part of its own past. Without this background, a distorted picture results—a record of Jewish experience with a gap that will hurt the self-understanding of American Jews. It cannot be omitted—it is a link in a long chain.

—MAX ROSENFELD
Philadelphia, April 1967

LEON KOBRIN

LEON KOBRIN

1872-1946

Leon Kobrin, pioneer of American-Yiddish letters, came to this country in 1892 at the age of 20. By 1910 a volume of his collected stories, all written here, ran to almost a thousand pages. In addition to short stories, he wrote a number of successful plays for the Yiddish stage, as well as several novels. (His *"Ora the Beard"* was one of the first full-length Yiddish novels written in this country.) His memoirs are a vivid record of a turbulent period of American-Jewish experience. Much of his time, in the early years, was spent in translating Russian and French novels into Yiddish; in this work he had the help of his wife, Pauline, who was a translator and critic in her own right.

His first literary attempts at the age of 15 were in Russian. Like many others of his generation, Kobrin had to learn how to use Yiddish as a literary instrument. Here in America he found a large and expanding audience for Yiddish and he was soon writing about Jews in all walks of life and in a great variety of situations.

A writer of the realist school, his stories are filled with details describing the people and places he came to know and love. A good many of his stories are concerned with the conflicts and disappointments of the young Jewish radicals who came to this country imbued with revolutionary ideals of building a new and just society. Better than some of the other Yiddish writers of his time, he succeeded in depicting the moments of intense love, anger and passion which moved his characters; gifted with a natural sense of drama, he was able to reveal the clash of forces in American Jewry through the experiences of the individual Jews who peopled his stories.

Kobrin was more than a pioneer in American Jewish literature. He laid a good part of the foundation, too. He was among the first of the intellectuals of his generation to note the emerging of a new Jewish group entity in the United States and he grappled with this phenomenon in his work.

A Common Language

by Leon Kobrin

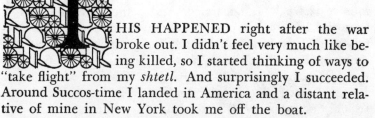HIS HAPPENED right after the war broke out. I didn't feel very much like being killed, so I started thinking of ways to "take flight" from my *shtetl*. And surprisingly I succeeded. Around Succos-time I landed in America and a distant relative of mine in New York took me off the boat.

Ai, the troubles of a greenhorn! A scholar in the subject of cloakmaking, as I am today, I had not yet become. And if in those days you had "unioned" me till you were blue in the face, I still would not have understood what a "unya" was or what "workers' interests" were or what "pickeven" meant. Although, to tell the truth, even in those days I knew how to smack a man in the mug so hard he'd see his grandmom in the next world. But I didn't know, as yet, that it was "scabs" you were supposed to smack. Back home in my *shtetl* I wasn't so choosy. Let somebody start up with me—smack! right in the teeth, and he'd turn over three times!

That's why, in fact, they used to call me "the wild animal." But they had more respect for *me* than for the rabbi—almost as much, maybe, as for the Russian constable.

I made my living selling fish in the market. From the other fishmongers, sneak-thieves used to swipe fish. But not from me! Never a single fishbone ever went astray on me—that's how much respect people had for my two fists. But here in America—no more bigshot. Nothing respected me, not even hunger. For days at a time I roamed the streets looking for ways to earn a few pennies, but it was no use.

I had brought a few dollars from home. But I am, unfortunately, a man who likes to eat. And your American bread isn't big enough to fill one of my teeth. And my teeth, thank God, are still all present in my mouth. So the few dollars quickly melted away.

And back home I had left a young wife. Pretty, too. Only four years we'd been married. And a three-year-old doll—a beautiful little girl. I thought about them all the time and missed them so much I thought I'd go crazy! I hadn't left them much money. What were they living on there? Suppose they didn't have enough to eat, God forbid? Twice a week I wrote a letter to my wife, and in every letter I told her, "Soon. Soon. Soon I'll be sending you some American dollars."

So *she* waited there and *I* waited here.

A month passed. Another month. I was starting to lose all hope of ever earning a penny in America.

I lived with a relative, a peddler, an out-and-out pauper with a houseful of little kids. So he advised me to go peddling, too. All right, I thought, let it be peddling! He even bought me a basketful of notions. Now go out, brother! Go forth and knock on doors! So I went forth and knocked . . . Knock

today, knock tomorrow. Knock and knock and with each door I felt like more and more of a *shlimmazl*. This one insulted me—how come a big strapping fellow like you goes around peddling? You're not strong enough to get a real job? And another answered me in Turkish or Hindu or whatever it was and go understand what she's saying! And in a third place they didn't say anything—slammed the door on my nose and—get lost!

Well, at the end of the week I gave my relative back his basket: "No more knocking on doors, Yosha. It's too much like begging. *They* don't buy and *I* don't sell. I'd rather go dig ditches or break rocks . . ."

And I started looking again. I looked and looked and found—nothing!

Inside my pockets a cold wind whistled. My stomach kept turning over, demanding its due. My relative and his wife felt very sorry for me. They couldn't bear to witness my troubles, they said, so would I please take pity on them and find myself new lodgings . . .

When I heard that, as you can imagine, I felt even better. Once in a while they would ask me to sit down and eat with them. But all the while I could see the black look in her eye, so I spared myself the misery of the meals, and instead, when they were all asleep in the middle of the night, your humble servant would slide silently off his bed of boards, tiptoe into the kitchen in his bare feet and—live it up!

At first the peddler's wife blamed her losses on the kids, but she soon caught on who the real culprit was and came at me in earnest. "It's not enough I give you a place to sleep, you have to eat me out of house and home! Who do you think I am—Mrs. Rothschild? I'm a poor man's wife and I have enough mouths to feed without yours!"

That same week I read an advertisement in the Yiddish paper that a certain cantor in Brownsville needed a basso.

Now I want you to know that back home, for the High Holidays, I used to help out the Reader in the synagogue. So I thought: If I can't dig ditches or break rocks—then let me try singing!

I borrowed a dime from my relative and rode out to Brownsville.

The cantor was a distinguished looking man with a high silk hat and a short-trimmed beard. I came right to the point. Such and such is my name. A basso from Russia. Sang with some of the leading cantors in Europe. And so forth. He asked me to sing something. I cleared my throat and let go a note with all my steam, like a locomotive. And—hoo-ha!— I gave out, brother, with all my tonsils. The cantor clapped both hands over his ears and screwed up his face in pain, as though I was beating him over the head with a blackjack.

"*Gevald! Gevald!* Enough! Stop!"

So I stopped.

"You sure can holler," he said. "You have, *k'n'hora,* a lot of strength. But singing—may God protect us!"

Well, what do you think happened? All of a sudden I felt tears streaming down my cheeks; hot, scalding tears. The first time in my life I ever bawled and blubbered like an old woman.

To make a long story short, the cantor, not a bad sort, started asking me questions and I told him everything.

"Listen," he said to me when I finished. "I think I know of a job for you. A rich member of my *shul,* a builder, needs a watchman." And without another word he picked up the telephone, called the builder, and told him the whole story.

"Tell him to come right over!" said the builder.

So in a little while I stood with the cantor in front of a rich house with two lions outside the door. The lions had their mouths open.

"Don't be afraid," joked the cantor. "They won't bite.

They're made out of stone."

"It would be better if they were real," I said. "Then they could make a meal out of me and that would be the end of it!"

We walked through the door and into the house. The place gleamed and sparkled. Big mirrors in golden frames. Pictures on the walls. Golden furniture. A big clock, also made of gold. Even the walls were decorated with gold stripes. The whole house was full of gold.

The builder himself, a short, jolly man, with a red beard and freckles and a sizable pot-belly, started right in. When did I come here, where did I come from, what did I do in the old country and so on and so on. I gave him straight answers to all his questions.

"Understand," he said, "I *had* a watchman. But he had one bad habit. He couldn't stay awake nights. So thieves came and stole things from my houses. Poor people live in that neighborhood, and they steal lumber, as much as they can carry away. So three days ago I sacked him. And now my wife and my son have to sit there all night long in the shack, like watchdogs . . ."

Then he asked me more questions.

"Can I depend on you?"

"Certainly."

"You won't fall asleep?"

"Sleep? Who can sleep in America?"

"You'll watch good?"

"What else? Of course!"

"Can you sock a man, if necessary?"

I didn't understand what he meant.

"With your fists, I mean. *Eylem-beylem, yamtsadreylem!* So the thief will see stars and stay ten miles away from my houses—"

"When it comes to that," I told him, "you can depend on

me. I'm not so much in love with the people here that I'll hold back a good punch if they need one!"

In short, I got the job. Ten dollars a week. And for that I had to watch the houses all night so nobody would steal anything. Before I left, the builder said to me:

"Remember now, no sleeping! Watch with both eyes and listen with both ears. Because my wife, God bless her, doesn't sleep too well herself. In the middle of the night she'll show up outside your shack. So remember—*eylem-beylem-yam-tsadreylem!* If a thief should come, give him the right translation of that verse!"

And that's how I became a night watchman in America.

* * *

The houses that I watched seemed far away from the rest of the world. All around was open field. The only lights I could see were in the distance. At night a frightening darkness crept over the field and the lights in the distant houses stared through the dark like the eyes of cats. Kroak-roak, the frogs sang in the swamps. Now and then a street-car clanged faintly, a long way off.

But that's only when the night was quiet and clear. Let a rain come down and a wind howl—then I would feel all alone and miserable in my little shack. The winds raged and yowled like cats battling in the darkness, or they shrieked and yammered like evil spirits. The rain beat down on the roof like peas dropping from a great height. And although by nature I don't scare easily, on such a night I would feel uncommonly gloomy. I was not accustomed to such a life, just sitting and listening, doing nothing. It made me nervous. Often I would feel that I was all alone in the world, cut off from everybody, surrounded by all the demons and goblins and evil spirits which had terrified me when I was a little boy. I was still a pious greenhorn, so I often turned to the old prayers and I would say the *krishma* and sometimes I even talked to myself out loud just to hear a human voice. Or I would burst into a cantorial piece with my big bass voice and almost scare myself to death.

Then I would get angry with myself. "You idiot! What's there to be afraid of?" And I would screw up my courage and go outside my shack to "inspect" the houses. But I was still afraid to look into the darkness where the awful voices howled, and I kept my eyes on the lighted window of my shack. Of human beings I was not afraid, not of the worst gangsters! But of the dark and the things that meowed there —that was a different story!

Luckily, however, the rain did not fall every night, nor the winds howl. On quiet nights the croaking of the frogs recalled my old home to me and I would think about my wife Hinda and my baby Esther. I missed them so much! I loved them more than ever before. Thinking about them would remind me that I was *not* all alone in the world, that back home I had a sweet, pretty wife who thought about me, too, and a bright little creature who called me Daddy. If only they were here with me in my shack, life wouldn't be so bad. Without them, however, life was bitter. Now that I had begun to earn money I felt even worse. You have a pretty wife but *she's* there and *you're* here. You have a cute baby and you can't even kiss her. But then I would remind myself that it would not be long before I'd be able to send them money. And I would cheer up.

The first week passed peacefully. Nobody came to steal. My boss's missus, a tall, skinny woman with a big mouth, almost every night seemed to grow out of the ground and knock at my window.

"Hey! You're not asleep?"

So I would come outside and she would hold her lantern

up to my face to see whether I hadn't been taking a nap, heaven forbid. Then she'd say:

"That's the way! Be a good worker and you'll amount to something in America!"

And off she'd go. Not once did she say "Good-night."

* * *

I came to hate her like poison. I had to bite my tongue to keep from telling her off. Her husband, on the other hand, with his red beard and freckles, was a regular guy, always cheerful. Sometimes he would slip me a cigar, "to help me pass the time."

"My missus sends regards! She told me to tell you—listen with your eyes and watch with your ears! And the main thing —remember that verse. In case, God forbid, a thief shows up, don't hesitate—*eylem-beylem-yamtsadreylem!*"

Until one night—

One night I sat in my shack "on duty." It was a Monday night, I remember, during the second week. In my pocket lay the first American dollars I had gotten from my boss that very day. My pocket was warm and so was my heart. I thought about my Hinda and imagined how she would open the envelope that I would send her and how she'd cry for joy. And for joy I felt like crying myself . . .

In my half-sleep I heard the croaking of the frogs, kroak-roak, kroak-roak, but suddenly, a new sound—cling-cling-cling—like nails spilling on wood—

I jumped up out of my chair. There were kegs of nails out there near the boards. Was he finally here, the gangster, the thief? I listened more intently. Again—cling-cling-cling. Then I heard something else—footsteps on the boards.

My heart skipped. Suppose it *was* a gangster and I'd now have to carry out my boss's verse—*eylem-beylem-yamtsadreylem?* The truth is, although I don't frighten easily, at that moment I *was* trembling a little. With an old-country thief I would have flown out of there like a bomb. With an American, however—who knows what kind of cutthroat was out there in the dark? Maybe he would teach *me* the verse —

So I carefully picked up my lantern and tiptoed out of the shack. The darkness was so thick you could almost put your hands on it. The distant little flames which at other times stared back at me like cat's eyes were now the eyes of dangerous American gangsters with knives and pistols in their pockets and axes in their hands.

I hesitated. Suddenly, out of *my* throat, came Russian words: *Kto-tam! Hey! Kto-tam!* Who's there?" In my fear, I must have forgotten where I was in the world.

No answer. I waited quietly again. Kroak-roak from the swamps and no other sound.

I yelled out again. Hey! *Kto-tam!* And my bass echoed so hollowly in the dark, so unfamiliar, as though another man stood behind me and bellowed.

I started to inch my way forward, holding my lantern in front of me. Suddenly—crack! The glass in the lantern shattered, the flame went out, a rock grazed my leg and landed behind me.

And that, you see, put an end to all my fears. I lunged at the pile of boards, screaming as though I were attacking all the gangsters in America at one time. I heard footsteps running across the boards and then—slam! a rock hit my right shoulder so hard it almost knocked me over. But that didn't stop me either. Not me! Nothing concerned me now but getting my hands on somebody—

But the gangsters must have sensed in my voice that I could take care of myself. Soon I heard them running away in the fields. They had retreated . . .

* * *

Later, when I returned to my shack, I felt a sharp pain in my shoulder, but my heart was a lot lighter than before. Because now I knew that American gangsters run away, too. In that case, I wasn't afraid of *them* either.

I unbuttoned my shirt to look at my wound. The skin was red as fire.

"Gangsters! Just wait! You'll pay for this! Let me only get you in my hands for one minute! I'll teach you the verse so well you'll never forget it—*eylem-beylem-yamtsadreylem!*"

In the morning we discovered that the gangsters had tried to make off with a keg of nails, but I had frightened them away just in time. They had left it in a ditch. My boss and his missus couldn't stop praising me.

"Did you at least teach them my verse?" he wanted to know.

And his wife, the tall skinny pest with the big mouth, beamed and said to him: "Didn't I tell you he would be a good cat for our mice?"

"You're a *better* cat, Rivkele . . ."

She didn't take this as a compliment. "Common peddler!" she muttered.

He laughed. "Don't take offense—" Then he turned to me. "Here—let me treat you to a schnapps! You've earned it!" And he handed me a dollar bill. But his wife, quick as a wink, snatched the money out of his hand.

"Look at him—Mister Big-hearted!" She hid the bill in her pocket, stuck a quarter in my hand and flounced away.

My boss laughed louder and jollier and said: "Women! What a nation! Who ever invented them?" He gazed after his wife, disappearing among the houses, took another dollar bill out of his pocket and slipped it to me on the sly.

"Here, take it! But if you ever catch one of them—"

I laughed, too. "It'll be just too bad for him! I'll translate your verse for him good! Don't worry!!"

"Exactly! That's what I mean exactly! Always keep my verse in mind! Understand? Not only in your mind—but in your fists!" And in a confidential, keep-a-secret tone, he continued: "I have an old, personal grudge against them. In the days when I was a peddler, they pestered the life out of me. And they're the same ones who come here to steal. So when you catch one of those loafers, let him have it, lay it on him good! No mercy! Beat him up! Twist his arm off! Break his leg! Knock his block off! In America you can even shoot at a thief. In short—*eylem-beylem yamtsadreylem!*"

And he ran off after his wife . . .

* * *

Another week went by. I sent my wife off a few dollars and in my head I had already figured out how much longer I would have to work before I could send her a big enough sum to open a little store there. And then the catastrophe hit me—

A terrible night. A cold rain. A bitter wind howled, whistled, barked, tried to turn the world upside down. It was an awful night to be out, and it was even worse all alone in my shack. Now it rattled and shook like a man in a fever, now it seemed as though the wind was about to pick it up and turn it over together with me and the iron stove at which I sat and warmed myself.

I thought I would feel better if I looked out the window. For a moment I saw nothing but the rain smashing against the glass. Suddenly—a little flame, moving out there in the dark! I stared. There it was again—a little red flame, moving slowly toward the boards. Aha! My guest was back!

"Gird your loins, Reb Bertchik!" I said out loud.

And I tightened the belt around my pants, rolled up my sleeves, and sharpened my weapons . . .

"Reb Bertchik, make them pay for that pain in your

shoulder, too!"

Quietly I stepped out of the shack, not a bit afraid now; it was like the good old days back home. And my temper was burning hotter inside me by the second.

Through the darkness I saw a lantern on the ground near a pile of boards. I bent over and made myself as small as I could. One step at a time, I moved closer and closer to the light.

The wind howled, the rain whipped my face and the cold went right through my bones.

Close enough now, I saw someone stooping over, poking around the boards. Silently I took a few more steps. Now I was right behind him. I tackled him, but so hard that he hit the ground with his face. I wrestled him up and wham! in the face. Bop! in the eye. Sock! in the teeth. Bang! I boxed his ears. And then I started all over again from the beginning.

The gangster started to scream for mercy. But I paid no attention. I went ahead with my lesson. *Eylem-beylem-yam-tsadreylem!* And I kept pounding it into him with both fists. Wham! Sock! Crack! A left! A right!

But here—what is this? Something was biting my knee and screaming in terror. Must be a dog. I yanked my leg away and reached for a stick, a board, anything to drive that mad dog away. But then I saw her—it was not a dog. It was a little girl. Five-six years old. The rain was pouring off her as she shook and trembled like a water-drenched kitten and cried and sobbed breathlessly, and shrieked and stared at me and stared . . . God in heaven! What eyes that little girl had and how she looked at me! The Angel of Death himself staring at me would not have upset me so much.

My tongue was struck dumb. My limbs refused to move. It was she, this little girl, who had screamed so terribly and who had bitten my leg as I beat the man—

The man—was he her father? But how could he have taken

her outdoors on such a night, especially when he had come to steal? Impossible that he was her real father!

But then she ran over to him as he lay groaning on the ground and fell on his neck and wept pitifully—and called him "Papa" . . . When I heard that, my heart broke. I thought I'd go out of my mind. God in heaven! So he's a thief. But a thief also has fatherly feelings! How could he have dragged such a baby along with him?

Now the man sat up and put his arms around the little girl and kissed her and comforted her and talked to her softly and talked and talked . . . I could see that he *did* love her, that he *was* behaving like a father. Then how—?

Suddenly it struck me. Maybe he had no home for himself and his child? Who knows what kind of place *Ameritchke* is? Maybe that's why he went out to steal on a night like this—?

A fire went through my brain. Maybe he had done it for the sake of his child—my hands ought to wither!

I picked up his lantern and went over to him. The little girl began to scream again, and kicked at me, and punched me with her little fists. The man, his face bloody, was trying to tell me something as he imploringly held out both his hands. My whole body began to tremble and I felt that I myself was about to start bawling. I began to talk to him— in Russian, in Yiddish, in Hebrew.

"Such a little girl, how could you—in such weather?"

Then *he* said something, and the child kept on crying, and the rain poured down, and the wind wailed . . .

"Don't cry, *liebinke,* don't cry, little girl! May my hands fall off if I hurt your father again!"

She didn't understand me. So I pulled a half-dollar out of my pocket and tried to put it into her little hand. But she threw the coin away from her onto the boards and kept on crying.

I started to look for the half-dollar with my lantern. The man had gotten up on his feet. He came over, picked up the coin and handed it to me. I pushed it back into his hand. Whereupon he let out a pitiful moan, like a whipped dog, and fell on my shoulder and kissed it.

I thought my heart would break to bits.

"Come," I said, pointing to the shack. He understood me. He said something to the child, and spoke to her soothingly until she grew quiet. Then he lifted her up into his arms and we all went inside the shack. I was ashamed to look into his eyes, he was so bloody and beaten.

I handed him a pail of water and a towel. And while he was washing his face, I looked at the girl who stood gazing forlornly at us both. How pale she was, how thin, and how amazingly large were her black, frightened eyes. I raised my hand to pet her, but she leaped away from me like a startled animal. I took a bagel out of my lunch-bag, smeared it with butter and offered it to her. She looked at it, and looked, and practically swallowed it with her eyes, but she refused to take it from me, from the gangster who had beaten her father so unmercifully . . .

* * *

In a little while, the man, an Italian in his forties, and his little daughter, sat at my stove and warmed themselves. We talked, he in his language, I—in mine.

He pointed to her dress, her shoes, showed me how skimpy and threadbare they were. We talked in sign language, with our hands, with gestures. But we understood each other; we understood each other very well, even though we didn't speak each other's language. He peddled bananas, he told me, and he had a wife and four bambinos, one younger than the other, and his house was cold, and he had come here to gather up some wood, and he had brought the little girl along to hold the lantern for him . . .

A thought seared my brain—maybe *my* house in the old country was cold, too? I deserved to be whipped! Why had I beaten him this way?

I handed him the bagel and pointed to the little girl. He gave it to her and she took it. When I saw how greedily she devoured it, I thought of my Estherke. Maybe my baby was going hungry, too?

I tried to talk with the girl.

"Good bagel, yes?"

She turned her head away.

"I not hurt your Papa again . . ." I tried to stroke her hair. But she stamped her little foot and hurled the bagel to the ground. She could not forgive me . . .

If somebody had beat *me* that way, my Estherke would not forgive him either . . .

After a while, the man took his daughter by the hand. "Now must go home," he explained.

"Wait!" I said. "Come with me!" I took them over to the pile of boards, gathered up a heap of kindling and put it into his arms.

"Now go!"

But out of the darkness and the cold rain—*mazl-tov! She's here!* The missus! As though sprung from the earth. In one hand an umbrella, which the wind was trying to tear out of her hand. In the other a lantern which she held up to my face, then at the man with his armful of kindling, then at the little girl standing by his side, and in her bewilderment she lost her tongue.

To tell the truth, when I saw her I was scared myself, at first. To come out of the dark unexpectedly like that! But soon I recovered myself and I pushed the man away.

"Go! Go!"

The missus dropped her umbrella and the wind caught it up and carried it off a little way until it caught on a board. But she grabbed the man's sleeve.

"What *is* this?" she barely managed to mutter.

"Kindling wood," I said. "You really don't need it. He's in trouble. His family's freezing. Look at that poor little girl . . ."

"*Ganef!*" she screamed at me. "This is how you watch our property? This is what we pay you for?"

"I'm not a thief, missus! For a word like that I usually hand out a smack in the teeth!" And I pulled her away from the man.

"Go!" I said again. "Go!"

He walked away quickly with the armful of kindling, his little daughter lighting the way ahead for him.

My missus apparently was afraid of *me* now. Because suddenly she started talking to me in a completely different tone, so soft, so soothing, like salve on a wound.

"Bertchik, dear Bertchik, let go my arm. You're hurting me, Bertchik. I have a weak heart. A strong man like you wouldn't know about such things. So you gave away some kindling. So what? We won't go bankrupt over it. You're a good man, Bertchik. You have a heart of gold. Let go my arm, Bertchik dear . . ."

So I let go her arm and she snatched up her umbrella.

"Good night!" she said, and vanished in the darkness. The first time since I'd been working there that she ever said good night to me!

* * *

The next morning she came to my shack with her husband and both of them had only one thing to say to me:

"You're fired!"

Later, walking toward the streetcar line with my bundle
under my arm, I bumped into my Italian friend on Pitkin
Avenue, standing next to a pushcart. He recognized me and
offered me a banana. I told him about *my* calamity in my
language, and he told me again about *his* troubles in his
language, and again we both understood each other. We understood each other very well indeed . . .

Bubba Basha's Turk

by Leon Kobrin

UBBA BASHA is a woman in her late fifties. Her *lantsleit* from Zlidnivka, who live here in New York, call her simply "Bubba." She has been in New York for three years and lives with a married daughter. She is a small woman with a bent back and a tiny, wrinkled face as big as a fist.

Every day, winter or summer, you could see her in her kerchief and quilted dress from the old country, with a gray cloth shawl draped over her shoulders, walking from Ludlow Street, where her daughter lives, to Monroe Street. On Monroe Street, outside a tobacco shop, stood a wooden Indian in a red Turkish fez. Bubba Basha would walk as far as the "Turk," count off two tenement house doors and go inside the third one. On the third floor of this house, in two rooms, lived old Reb Boruch, her *lantsman*. Bubba liked to visit with his wife Ethel, to whom she confided everything that was accumulating inside her troubled heart.

"The children aren't Jews . . . Why did I have to drag my old bones to this hell, God forgive me . . . Oh, Ethel, may

He not punish me for the thought—why didn't I die there, at least I would be near my Moishe and not see the terrible things that go on here!"

Ethel would sigh, too, and eventually the two women would start on "America" and pour out all their wrath upon it. After a few hours, Bubba Basha would take her leave of her *lantsfroi* and go back home, following the same route past the "Turk." She would count off several streets from the Turk, turn into East Broadway and count off another few streets until she came to Ludlow. There, outside a fish-store, hung a big golden fish. From the golden fish to her house was only a few doors.

Exactly how old Bubba was no one knew, not even she herself. When they asked her: "Bubba, how old are you?" she would figure it out this way: "May it never happen to anyone here, to any Jew, but before the first cholera epidemic I must have been about five years old. And a year before the first big fire—when I was about thirteen—I got married. And after the second big fire I already had Mirele. And when my father—may he be a good pleader for us in the next world—took his second wife, I already had had Boruch. And Boruch, *olev hasholom*, died a good forty years ago. And when my father, may we never hear of such things, took sick, I already had Zelda. And when he died, God grant us long years, I was then pregnant with Chaim. . . ."

Her whole life had been spent in Zlidnivka with her husband, Reb Moishe Tsivia's (his mother's name was Tsivia), or Moishe the Lame, as most people called him. She bore his children, buried some of them, raised the rest of them, and never set foot outside her *shtetl*. Life paraded before her with all its joys and sorrows, but Bubba never noticed it. There had to be a plague, a fire, a wedding, an illness, a crisis, before Basha had any sense of being alive. So these were the events by which she measured her life.

Two years after her husband's death, her children sent her two steamship tickets for America, for her and her *lantsman,* who would bring her here.

Bubba Basha was not pleased with America. The children did not practice their religion; the houses all looked alike—big and shapeless; the streets had such weird names—she defied anyone to pronounce them. The only saving grace was that the Almighty had given human beings brains and in a time of need they came to one's aid. For instance, the sign of the Golden Fish and the Wooden Turk. Were it not for them, she would never have been able to find her way to Reb Boruch's.

Pesach time, Bubba Basha refused to eat at her daughter's table, even though her daughter "kept kosher." It was obvious that her daughter's house was not *Pesachdik* enough. So her children were forced to pay Reb Boruch for her meals during the Passover holiday. The first Pesach things worked out fine. But on the second one, when Bubba was on her way to Reb Boruch's for the *seder,* a terrible misfortune happened.

Let Bubba Basha tell that story in her own way.

The heart of man knows many thoughts, my Moishe used to say. (May he have a glorious Paradise!) So that if one is destined to suffer a misfortune—it should never happen here, it should never happen to any Jew—no earthly wisdom can prevent it. . . .

Who could have expected it? All year long—praise His Name—I walk to Reb Boruch's house without any trouble. But exactly one hour before the *seder* this terrible thing had to happen to me! As usual, I went out into the street, I came to the Golden Fish and I counted three streets and walked ahead. And praised be God, I came to the street where that train is pulled by those big horses. Then I walked four more crooked streets and turned into another crooked street and again I counted five crooked streets and came into the one where Reb Boruch lives.

And that is where the Turk should have been. I looked for him—but no Turk! Well, I thought, I must have made a mistake about the street, and I turned around and went to another crooked street and I looked again. Nothing. No sign of the Turk. Would I at least have seen a Jew to ask for directions! But that I could not do either—who can recognize a Jew here, when every man has hacked off his beard?

So I stood and waited, maybe God would send me help—praised be His Name—but there was no sign of a Jew. What could I do? And here it was growing later and later. I would never be at Reb Boruch's in time for the *seder*. My heart grew bitter and dark. What has happened to you, I said to myself. You went and dragged your old bones to such a God-forsaken America, and now, a few minutes before the first *seder*, you're standing in the middle of the street and who knows what will happen, praise God. I couldn't control myself any longer and began to cry. Suddenly I saw a Jew with a black beard running toward me. Thank God, I thought, finally, at last, one Jew!

"Reb Yeed," I said, "long life to you, can you maybe tell me where I am? I'm lost . . ."

The Jew stopped, took a look at me and asked: "Where do you want to go, bubba?"

"I want to go to Reb Boruch's house. Woe is me, Reb Yeed, you'll earn a *mitzva*! I'll be late for the *seder*, please!"

"Where does Reb Boruch live, bubba?"

"Near the Turk, please help me, you'll earn a *mitzva*!"

The man took another look at me and ran away.

"Reb Yeed! Have pity!" I called out after him. But it was none of his business.

I was in great trouble. What would happen to me!

But coming toward me was a group of men with shaven

faces. And one of them stopped and asked me, in Yiddish: "Bubba, why are you standing here in the middle of the street?"

My voice trembled so, I could hardly answer him. "If you still have a Jewish heart, take pity on a poor old woman!"

"What do you want, bubba?"

"Woe is me, I'm lost!"

"Where do you want to go, bubba?"

"Take pity on me, please, show me where Reb Boruch lives. He comes from Zlidnivka, he's a *melamed,* and he lives near the Turk. Show me where the Turk is and you'll earn a *mitzva!*"

The shaven faces had a good laugh (God grant they laugh out of the other side of their mouths!) and then one of them said to me:

"It's too long a trip to Eretz Yisroel, bubba!"

And another one said: "After Pesach we'll go with you!"

And a third said: "It's a shame to leave the *kneydlech* here, bubba!"

By this time there was a whole crowd around me, men, women, children, watching me and making fun of me. Woe is me! Then a policeman came; a man said something to him, pointing to his own forehead. The policeman asked me something. I did not understand him and I began speaking to him in Russian.

Everybody burst out laughing again. Devils! The policeman took me by the arm and started to drag me away. The children ran after me, screaming "hurray!" and I screamed to the shaven faces—

"Brothers! Save me from Gentile hands!"

But they only laughed, and the policeman kept on dragging me.

In short, they brought me to the police-station, and there a group of policemen gathered around and laughed at me.

And all the time it was getting later and later. I wept at my bitter fate. And then one policeman startled me by asking me a question in Yiddish. In the midst of my tears I answered him.

"I'm a decent woman. I haven't stolen anything, as God is my witness. I was only on my way to Reb Boruch the *melamed* who lives near the Turk and I lost my way and nobody helped me and the policeman came and brought me here. But why? What did I do?"

"Where does Reb Boruch live?" he asked me.

"Near the Turk, I just told you, near the Turk," I said.

"Who is this Turk you keep talking about and what does he look like?"

"How should he look? Like a Turk!"

The policeman laughed. "How do you know he's a Turk? Does he walk around the street in Turkish clothes?"

"How can he walk around? He's made of wood."

The policeman laughed out loud and said something to the others and they almost went into convulsions—may we never know of such things. Then the policeman who spoke Yiddish took me out into the street to look for the Turk. We walked and walked and at last the policeman stopped at a store with a big sign in the window. He studied the sign for a minute and then said to me:

"Yesterday there was a tobacco shop here. Was your Turk standing here?"

And just then my daughter—good health to her—came running toward us. The world brightened up and I burst out crying in sheer happiness.

"Where were you, Mama? Ethel came to find out why you didn't come to the *seder* and we've been running all through the streets looking for you! We realized you must be lost when we saw the tobacco shop empty and the Turk gone . . ."

And I? I wept for joy and couldn't stop . . .

Little Souls

by LEON KOBRIN

OME YEARS AGO I worked for a short time in a cigar factory that did not hire Jewish "hands." Although the factory was practically "one of our own"—it belonged to one of our brothers in Israel, a German Jew—nevertheless, the foreman of the factory, Mr. McCarthy, an Irish gentleman, would always send a Jewish worker, if such would ever come looking for a job, "to Jerusalem." And at the same time he would also remind him—the Jewish worker—to "take his whiskers with him."

Devil take that dear Mr. McCarthy, that's the kind of fanatical Zionist *he* was!

How did it happen, then, that he hired *me?* I can't give you the real answer to that question. Most likely he took me for a Spaniard, because I do somewhat resemble one of Torquemada's *lantsleit,* and then again, I came in asking for work on "Spanish cigars." Whatever the case may be, Mr. McCarthy hired me and that's the main thing.

So I sit between two Germans and I work. The work is good; the material is outstanding. I am turning out fine cigars . . .

Mr. McCarthy is a short, thick-set man in his forties, clean-shaven, with thin lips, a red nose and a massive mug, with a thick, powerful neck and a big, round head which looks almost bald because the hair is clipped so close. He stands at a separate table near the window, a leather shade over his eyes, a short, black apron around his middle, his sleeves rolled up, and packs the cigars into boxes. And as he packs the cigars, his mouth keeps moving like a windmill, grinding out one joke after another, at which the workers, naturally, laugh hilariously, whether the joke is funny or not. Because Mr. McCarthy, you understand, always laughs loudly himself at his own jokes, a boisterous laughter that reverberates through the factory like the braying of a jackass. And since he himself thinks his jokes are sidesplitting, the workers, of course, agree with him . . .

Among the cigarmakers around me I recognize two other "unofficial" Jews who have smuggled themselves into this place. One of them is a slender young fellow with a long, skinny neck, red hair and freckles, with a thin red moustache over his lip, and with tiny clever eyes which dart here and there from the board on which he rolls his cigars, to the pile of finished cigars at his hand, to his neighbor's pile, to the pile of the worker across from him, and then to Mr. Mc-Carthy. His eyes skip about ceaselessly as his skinny neck turns in every direction and his narrow shoulders and his arms move mechanically, as quickly and unceasingly as his eyes.

With a flick of the knife on the wrapper, a turn of his neck and shoulders, a glance of his leaping eyes around the work-board, he slides the unfinished cigars from the paper, touches it to his lips, slips it into the wrapper with two fingers, then deftly rolls it. All the time his fingers are moving nimbly in front of him as though he were playing a piano. Chop off the end with the cutter, smooth down the head of the cigar with his lips, toss it onto the pile of finished cigars, and his fingers never stop their "piano-playing" and his eyes keep skipping in all directions like the eyes of a mouse peering out of its hole . . .

The second "unofficial" Jew sits across from him on the other side of the table. He is a stout young man with a round smooth-shaven face and big round eyes always serious and puzzled-looking, as though his black curly head was crammed full of difficult world problems. This young man is a slow worker, inspects every leaf of tobacco on all sides before he starts to roll it, tries it carefully with his knife, and when he rolls the cigar he leans his chest against the table and barely moves his fingers. And all the while he sweats and gasps like a goose.

These two unofficial Jews always avoid one another, never look at each other, like that foolish bird which hides from an enemy by sticking his head under his wings, deducing that since he does not see his enemy, his enemy will not see *him*. Devil only knows why they refuse to recognize each other! But apparently they think that once they exchange a word, Mr. McCarthy will know they are Jews and send them both packing to Jerusalem. Naturally, they avoid me, too. One Jew can always spot another even when he looks like a Spaniard!

At Mr. McCarthy's jokes these two unofficial Jews laugh even louder than the other cigarmakers. The redhead, the skinny one with the tiny leaping eyes, squeaks in a thin little voice and is always the first to laugh at the foreman's joke.

And as he laughs he squeals out the word "Jesus." The other one laughs in thick gasps, in deep, hoarse tones, as though the sounds were bursting out of his belly. And through it all his eyes never change their expression of earnest puzzlement. Often he laughs, not even knowing what he is laughing at. What's the difference? Everybody else is laughing, he might as well get into the act. And sometimes it happens that when all the others have finished laughing he realizes he has not even started yet and he looks up at Mr. McCarthy with an expression that says, "I swear, your Excellency, I didn't hear you!"

Often, Mr. McCarthy begins to spew out jokes about Jews, silly jokes, stale jokes, unfunny wisecracks full of venomous idiocy. Both of them laugh now, too, the red-headed young man even harder than usual; you can hear his squeals all over the factory, as he jumps out of his skin to make sure everyone has heard him and seen him holding his sides and stamping his feet. The laughter of the other one, the stout one, at times like this sounds a little unnatural—"Excuse me, I'm laughing, but I don't really feel like it . . ."

Poor little souls, in their laughter they try to hide from themselves!

Once a week they permit themselves to look at each other —the half hour on Saturday morning between eleven-thirty and twelve, when the Boss himself, "Brother" Weisberg, a solidly-built individual with a prominent nose, comes to the factory to distribute the pay envelopes. He strolls among his workers with a pleasant smile on his unmistakably Jewish face and lays an envelope beside each worker. Then the two unofficial Jews look at each other and their faces light up with a kind of ecstasy, as though they were signaling to each other: "One of ours, a brother in Israel!" At that moment they seem to look about them more boldly, more freely, more proudly. They feel like relatives to the factory, close relatives. But soon Brother Weisberg leaves the shop, and that's the end of it.

Day after day I sit and watch this tragi-comedy in the cigar factory. Sometimes I feel sorry for these two unofficial Jews; I try to excuse them—a man will do anything for his piece of daily bread. Sometimes I feel only bitter anger—especially when they laugh hysterically at Mr. McCarthy's anti-Semitic "jokes."

Things went along that way for several months. A few weeks before Christmas the place became extremely busy. Mr. McCarthy needed more hands. He advertised in the papers. Cigarmakers applied, but not as many as were needed. Among those that answered the want-ad was a Jew with a yellow, tangled beard and nearsighted eyes. He came into the shop with his tools wrapped in newspaper under his arm, took off his hat and remained standing at the door with a woebegone look on his face, his eyes peering in the direction of Mr. McCarthy.

The other workers took one look at the yellow, tangled beard and the yellow disheveled hair on his head, and burst into tumultuous guffaws.

And our "unofficial" ones? At first, when they saw him, they were flustered, even frightened. But immediately, the skinny one came to his senses and let out one of his squeals:

"Solomon Isaac, bejeezus!"

And the stout one bent his face until it almost touched the table, as though he were afraid the tangled-bearded Jew would notice his presence, and laughed his thick, grating laugh, and his big round eyes, as usual, filled up with a look of intense concentration.

McCarthy assigned the newly-hired hands to their places and when he finished with them he fixed his eyes on the Jew with the yellow tangled beard, who was still standing at the door with a beseeching look on his face. Mr. McCarthy rubbed his hand across his massive mug and bellowed: "Hollo, viskers! You vunt verk? Not here! Go to Jerusalem!" And he exploded with laughter at his own joke, he doubled up in hilarity, and his big body shook all over, and his coarse red face grew redder and redder, and his eyes teared and he neighed lustily and wildly like a well-fed stallion in heat.

The workers, naturally, supported him with a laughing chorus of their own, and the two "unofficials" did not stint their support either, and the whole shop resounded with such merriment that the bearded Jew at the door who had evoked all this fun smiled, too—a pitiful, sorrowful smile. Finally he put his hat back on his head, bowed low, said goodbye, bowed again, and backed out of the door like a thief.

"Don't forget to take your whiskers with you!" Mr. McCarthy yelled after him. Again a gale of laughter.

The next morning Mr. McCarthy's want-ad was in the papers again, again a few hands responded, and again the yellow-bearded Jew was among them. Mr. McCarthy again dispatched him cheerily to Jerusalem.

The fourth time around he hired him. He couldn't help himself. The Christmas orders had to be filled, even if the devil himself had to make the cigars!

But still, he couldn't resist the opportunity for one of his jokes.

"What's your name?"

"Nochem Treitle," replied the Jewish cigarmaker with a low bow.

"Nokim Treylik!" repeated Mr. McCarthy and his jowls shook in silent laughter. "Nokim Treylik! I ought to send you to Jerusalem to wash your hands, but I'm too busy!"

Nochem Treitle understood only enough English to know that Mr. McCarthy had said something about being "busy" and he said: "I make a cigar—a *tsatske!*" And afraid that the foreman might not have understood him, he began to roll his fingers. "First class cigar!"

When the two "unofficials" saw that he had been hired, their faces froze and they stared at him in helpless defeat.

It was my fate that Nochem Treitle should be seated next to me. He sat down to work and worked with such fervor, with his near-sighted eyes so close to the table, that his face was hardly visible, only his head of tousled yellow hair, the back of his yellow-fuzzed neck and the dirty collar of his shirt. All morning he worked without letup, in one breath, without even taking a moment to straighten his back.

Not until twelve o'clock, when all the workers stopped for lunch, did he also put down his tools and pick up a paper bag from beneath his chair. He put his old, begrimed hat on his head, opened up the bag, murmured the blessing and began to eat. He ate quickly—a piece of cake with cheese filling—and washed it down with milk from a little bottle. All the time he never moved his eyes from the pile of cigars he had completed. You could see him counting them in his mind. Then he looked around at his neighbors and recognized at once that I was a "brother in Israel." His eyes lit up and when I answered in the affirmative he asked me other questions about the shop and the cigarmakers who worked there.

I gave him straight answers and he was very pleased. At that point he took a good look at the skinny, redhaired young fellow who was sitting near us eating his lunch. Almost leaping from his chair, he called out excitedly: "Bentzi! You here, too! How are you, Bentzi?"

Bentzi shivered like a man in fever and the food dropped out of his mouth. His leaping eyes darted around the room. But nobody had noticed; the others were too busy with their newspapers and their conversation. Except the stout young man. He hid his head behind the table and scratched the back of his neck. The red-head regained his composure, stared at Nochem Treitle blankly and asked in a low voice: "What did you say?"

"Don't you recognize me?" demanded Nochem, speaking Yiddish. "You've gone crazy, or what? Don't you know me, Bentzi?"

"What the hell are you talking about? Talk United States!"

"My! My!" said Nochem Treitle, turning to me. "Listen to the clever one! Talks English like he was born to it! My *lantsman*—we came over on the same ship!" He turned back to Bentzi. "Remember, Bentzi, how you ate up all my lemondrops! Oh, were you seasick!"

But Bentzi had no intention of understanding him, even if you killed him for it. The end of the lunch period saved him from further danger, but he went back to his work with a kind of despair in his face and kept his eyes turned away from Nochem Treitle. Nochem didn't say another word either—just scratched his tangled yellow beard, bent over the table with a puzzled look in his nearsighted eyes and worked away at his cigars.

Every day was now an event. Every day, Mr. McCarthy and the workers had a free comic show. First of all, McCarthy picked on Nochem's cigars. Not made right. Not finished right. Actually, they were better shaped and better finished than the cigars being turned out by the other workers. And when Mr. McCarthy kept telling him that his cigars were only good enough for Jerusalem, Nochem could only stare at him with a hapless expression on his face, like a criminal caught redhanded and expecting the worst.

The workers naturally laughed at his terror-stricken look, and Mr. McCarthy, to frighten him still more, would mockingly challenge him to "fight" as he waved his powerful fists under Nochem's nearsighted eyes. And the laughter would grow louder and louder. And Bentzi would squeal and hold his sides and the stout young man with the look of wonderment in his eyes would nearly choke laughing.

And Nochem Treitle? He would look confusedly at Mr. McCarthy's hammerlike fists and tremble and blink his eyes and smile with a smile that was akin to silent weeping.

Whenever this happened I could barely sit still. I felt personally insulted for this Jew, for this human being, for this fellow-worker, who was being so humiliatingly degraded in the unfortunate person of Nochem Treitle. When I advised him once not to let people spit in his face this way, he said: "Eh! I should feel insulted because of a Gentile pig? What can I do? A Jew is in Exile." He shrugged his shoulders. "Let him do whatever he wants, as long as he lets me work here . . ."

But the longer he worked there the more they laughed at him. One day at lunch-time a German worker stuck a piece of ham into Nochem's hand. The shop became a real circus when the other workers noticed how Nochem Treitle hurled the ham away from himself violently as though it were a hot coal.

Every once in a while the foreman would pull Nochem's beard and say in mock politeness: "How do you do, Nock Treylik!" And then one day Mr. McCarthy came back from lunch drunk. Gleefully he patted Nochem on the shoulder and said, "How do you do, Nock!" and grabbed hold of his yellow, tangled beard and pulled Nochem down to his knees. And Nochem, going down to the ground, looked up at Mr. McCarthy out of his nearsighted eyes and said nothing. His whole face contorted as he tried to smile.

"Look at whiskers, boys, he's laughing!" Mr. McCarthy was enjoying himself.

I leaped from my chair half-crazed with anger and humiliation. "Bentzi! Moishe!" I cried out in Yiddish. "Say something! Who cut out your tongues! They're hurting a Jew! You're Jews yourselves!"

The shop grew suddenly still. McCarthy let go Nochem's beard. The cigarmakers all turned to look at me. Bentzi and the other one sat paralyzed, their faces burning, their eyes frantic. Only Nochem Treitle moved, looking around at everyone and grinning grotesquely.

"What the hell are you jabbering about?" Mr. McCarthy asked me.

"Leave the poor man alone!"

"Oho! So you're a Jew, too!"

"Yes! a Jew!" And I hit him full force in the face.

Taken completely by surprise, he looked at me dumbly, but then came charging at me with his fists up. I braced myself, but suddenly he turned on Nochem Treitle and picked him up bodily.

"Get out, godammit! And don't come back till Saturday for your pay!"

Nochem's face grew white as chalk as he packed up his tools. He kept looking at Bentzi. His lips and his yellow tangled beard trembled as he whispered: "Bentzi, put in a good word for me!"

Bentzi, of course, didn't even hear him.

With his bag of tools under his arm, Nochem Treitle left the shop as though in a drunken stupor.

I sat down and packed my cigars, counting them calmly, and then picked up my tools.

"I want my pay now," I said to McCarthy, trying to keep my voice steady.

And Mr. McCarthy, to my surprise, as though someone were holding a gun at his side, walked across the room with me, told the girl in the office to pay me, and returned to the shop without another word to me or anyone else.

But as I stepped out of the building—crack! something heavy hit me across the shoulders, once, twice. I whirled around. It was Nochem Treitle, swinging his pack of tools, his face twisted in anger, his whole body shaking in fury.

"Nochem! What—"

"You bastard!" he cried between his clenched teeth. "Damn you! Such a good job! Who asked you to worry about my beard? Damn you! Couldn't stand to see another Jew making a living! Such a good job! You bastard!"

ZALMAN LIBIN

ZALMAN LIBIN

1872-1955

Zalman Libin (Israel Hurwitz), like many other Jewish immigrants, worked in London first, before coming to the United States. After spending seven months there, he then settled in New York, where he worked as a capmaker for three years. He had written a few articles in Russian, but here in the United States he turned to Yiddish, writing for the ARBEITER TSEITUNG and the FORVERTS.

"*A Workingman's Sigh*," published in 1892, was the first Yiddish short story printed in this country, and the names of Libin and Kobrin are usually mentioned together as the pioneers of Yiddish literature in America. The villains of Libin's stories were the sweatshop boss and the landlord; the heroes and heroines, the Jewish sweatshop workers and their families.

"Do you know what it means to be unemployed in America?" asks one of his characters. "Do you know what it means to be without a job in Columbus's *medina?* Better you shouldn't. The earth slips away from under your feet, and overhead, instead of a sky, a hopeless gloom spreads out. For the rest of the world the sun shines, but not for the unemployed. Other people know the difference between ordinary days and holidays. For the unemployed there is no difference between one day and another. For him, every day is alike, molded from the same piece of black lead . . "

In an autobiographical note, Libin explained that he wrote about the Jewish working-people of New York "because that is the life I know best . . . In the gloomy sweatshop my muse was born; her first cry of pain was heard near the Singer machine; she grew up in the dark tenements; where she will die I don't know. Apparently in one of the same dark tenements, if she doesn't receive an eviction-notice first!"

Evidently Libin was able to laugh his "gloomy muse" out of countenance when the need arose—and there was always a need on the part of his readers to laugh. . .

My First Theft

by ZALMAN LIBIN

ALL MY LIFE, ever since I can remember myself as belonging to the human species, I have always had trouble keeping an umbrella—either I would forget it somewhere, or somebody would steal it. Sometimes this thievery would be carried out so brazenly, so flagrantly, that it would really unnerve me. One moment my umbrella would be standing at my side— I'd turn my head for a moment—gone! No more umbrella! As though evil spirits were playing games with me. And if I lost my patience and began yelling "Thieves! Robbers!," people would look at me and laugh, as though umbrellas were free public property . . .

I was never what you would call a rich man. The cheapest umbrella a self-respecting man can carry on a rainy day costs at least a dollar, and the longest period an umbrella would stay with me was two weeks, so you can understand that I couldn't afford to keep on buying umbrellas all my life. Things came to such a pass that my wife, God bless her, finally forebade me once and for all from buying umbrellas.

"No more umbrellas!" she decreed. "That's the last one! It's not my responsibility to supply the whole world with umbrellas!"

And although I knew that my wife was perfectly right, I still tried to put up a defense: "But how can I get along without an umbrella? What'll I do in a sudden downpour?"

"You'll stay home!"

"But what if I happen to be out at the time? Or if it happens that I must go out into the rain on important business?"

"You're not made out of sugar, my dear husband, you won't melt!" And that was her final verdict.

Whatever my Shifra decrees is carried out. For a long time there was not even a hint of an umbrella in our house, as though all the umbrellas in the world had been abolished. More than once I was caught in the rain and came home soaked to the skin. So what? It was nothing, really. During the storm I suffered. While the rain soaked me I was good and sore at my wife. But when I came home and dried out and realized that I hadn't lost my umbrella, that nobody had gotten a gift of an umbrella at my expense, then I used to feel so good that I wholeheartedly approved my wife's anti-umbrella policy.

And then it came to pass, we had some kind of holiday, and in honor of this holiday I dressed myself up in my new clothes—a new suit, a new hat, and brand new shoes which I hadn't even worn yet. My wife almost burst with pleasure looking at me.

"It must be true what the world says: Clothes make the man. You really look like one!" Which made me almost burst with pleasure, too.

At that moment—the words were on the tip of my tongue —I wanted to say: "But how can I go out without an umbrella when I'm dressed up like this in all my new things?" However, not wishing to spoil her good mood, I kept quiet.

But I happen to be an unlucky man. I went out for a walk, and it was such a pleasant day, and I walked and walked . . . and of course, down came the rain, a real flood, and I got soaked to my bones, and the black dye ran out of my new hat and down my face, and what happened to my new suit—I'd rather not even think about! And my new shoes shrank so much there was no room for my toes and all the way home I could hardly keep from crying.

When I finally did get home and my Shifra took one look at the beautiful end of all my beautiful new things, she wanted to kill herself.

No doubt you understand how miserable I felt. But when I saw how badly *she* felt, I forgot all about myself. Dear Father in heaven, how she carried on! It was a pity just to look at her . . .

But sometimes, out of the greatest misfortune, comes a blessing.

The next morning, my Shifra herself went out to the store and bought me an umbrella. However, when she handed me my present, she delivered the following ultimatum: "Here's a new umbrella for you," she began, her eyes flaming like two coals. "Here! Now you have an umbrella again! But listen, you unlucky scatterbrain! If anything happens to it, God help you! If you lose it, don't bother coming home! Remember—guard it with your life!"

So you can understand how I guarded that umbrella. Whenever I took it out with me I held on to it as though the whole world was out to steal it. Whenever I walked along the street with my Shifra's present in my hand I was afraid to think of anything else, lest I absent-mindedly leave it behind somewhere, God forbid. Whenever I went into a house or a store or wherever, nobody could persuade me to let go of it. And whenever anyone spoke to me, I didn't look at the speaker but at my umbrella. In short, I was so jittery about my umbrella that sometimes I thought I must be suffering from a new kind of hallucination called umbrellaphobia.

One rainy day I went outdoors, naturally with my umbrella in my hand, and happened to stop into a restaurant. I sat down at a table, ordered a cup of coffee, and, as usual, didn't let the umbrella out of my hand. A waiter came by, pointed to the puddle my umbrella was making on the floor, then pointed politely to a corner especially equipped for just such rainy days. There was nothing I could do, short of making a scene—which is not in my nature—and, willingly or no, I had to get up and stand my umbrella among its fellows.

I had planned to wait in that restaurant until the rain stopped, but because the umbrella was not safe in my hand, I began to feel uneasy. True, I didn't take my eyes off Shifra's present, and any time a diner got up to leave the restaurant I also got up and went to the umbrella stand, but, nevertheless, I couldn't stay in that restaurant very long. I felt apprehensive, as though my heart were warning me of an impending calamity, and as soon as I finished my coffee I got up to leave.

You can imagine my terror when I reached for my umbrella—and discovered it wasn't there! The world turned dark before my eyes! There *was* an umbrella in the stand, but it wasn't mine. The handle was *almost* like mine—but still not mine. My umbrella was a plain, dollar umbrella—the one in the stand was genuine silk and must have cost at least a fiver.

The thought went through my head: Perhaps somebody

made a mistake and exchanged umbrellas with me and I ought to ask the waiters if they knew who might have made the mistake. But then my heart skipped in fear—wouldn't I only make things worse with my questions? Maybe this umbrella belonged to someone who was still in the restaurant. Maybe my umbrella had really been stolen.

As I stood there at the umbrella-stand confused by my own thoughts, I was overpowered by a sudden desire to take that remaining umbrella and flee the restaurant—in other words, I was prepared to commit a theft. Morally I felt justified. My conscience would not bother me a hair even if I stole fifty umbrellas. On the contrary, I would feel good about committing such thefts—and I would prefer not to make any use of them whatever. Just give them out as gifts, break them up, tear them to bits, so long as I could take other people's umbrellas as they had taken mine! Let other people know how it feels to have your umbrella stolen right from under your nose! My heart and my soul commanded me to take that silk umbrella. But between the wish to steal and the actual deed there is a tremendous gap . . .

When I put out my hand to touch the umbrella, my hand became paralyzed, refused to move. My eyes began to smart, my head to swim. And finally, when I had forced myself to take it, a cold sweat broke out all over me and I knew the real taste of dying. I felt the eyes of everyone in the restaurant upon my hands, my face. I could hear people running toward me, screaming: "Thief! Keep your hands off! That's not yours!" They were already upon me, beating me, knocking me down. The blood pounded in my temples, my face grew hot and flaming, my limbs shook.

How I ever got out of there with that umbrella I'll never know. I have lost all memory of that act, as though I had been unconscious. I came to my senses only when I was several blocks away. I held my breath and looked behind me.

Strangely, no one was chasing me, no one was screaming *"Stop Thief!"* But my teeth chattered anyway.

Somehow I managed to walk to my street. There was our house. I calmed down a little, caught my breath. And suddenly I was exalted by a feeling of perfect happiness. I felt as though I had taken revenge on an enemy who had plagued and persecuted me all my life.

I studied the stolen goods. A genuine silk umbrella. Almost gleefully I entered my house, ready to astound my wife with the story of my bold adventure. She greeted me excitedly at the door.

"Simpleton! Did you bring back Sokolov's umbrella?" She glanced at the umbrella in my hand and sighed in relief. "Thank God! I thought you might have lost it . . ."

"Sokolov's umbrella?" I asked, bewildered. "What are you talking about?"

"Shlimmazl! Instead of taking your own umbrella when you went out, you took Sokolov's—he left it here last night!"

It was true. There was my own umbrella hanging on a nail in the hallway. I had stolen an umbrella from myself! All my anguish and torment at the restaurant had been for nothing. Well, not exactly for nothing. One thing had become very clear to me. I could never make my living as a thief . . .

Apples

(an adaptation)

by ZALMAN LIBIN

SLOWLY, STOPPING every once in a while, the horse pulled the wagonful of apples up the street. Behind the wagon walked a man of about forty and a boy of twelve. The man was the owner, the boss of the wagon, and the boy was a hired helper who hawked the wares and carried the apples up to the customers.

It was the end of a day at the beginning of winter. The weather was bad, gloomy; a cold, cutting wind had blown all day, bringing with it a fine, cold drizzle which penetrated the clothing and left people cold and damp.

A light summer jacket and a pair of light kneepants hardly protected the boy from the weather. The pants were so tattered that in many places his bare skin was exposed, and his toes stuck out of the torn shoes. He trembled and shook with the cold. And perhaps also from hunger. His small thin face was pale and blue with the cold.

"Five cents a quarter-peck!" shouted the boss in a kind of breathless way.

"Hey, apples," piped the boy in a hoarse, thin, heart-rending tone.

But nobody wanted any apples, and the horse took a step forward.

"Will we go home soon?" the boy asked the boss, his teeth chattering.

The boss had had a bad day's business and he didn't even deem it necessary to answer the boy's question.

"Apples! Five cents a quarter-peck!"

"Hey! Apples!"

"Will we go home soon?" asked the boy again.

The boss threw a slow, sharp, angry look at the boy and his face filled with a savage satisfaction, as though he wanted to make up for the day's bad business with the pleasure of watching his hired hand suffer.

"If I had known you were such a lazy kid," he barked, "I wouldn't even have hired you for nothing!"

"I'm not lazy, I'm cold," the boy defended himself tearfully.

"Cold?" the boss mimicked. "What's that to me? You'll want your quarter anyway! Hey! Apples! Get your apples! Five cents!"

The horse stepped along slowly, a few yards at a time. The boy's legs felt weak and he held on to the wagon. This was Sammy's first day as a huckster's helper. Previously, he had peddled newspapers. Sammy's father peddled suspenders. His mother he barely remembered. She had died when he was five. But he did have a stepmother. He also had a sickly little sister of his own, and three little half-brothers who belonged to his stepmother. But his father now had a wife

and five children, and on the money he earned as a suspenders-peddler there was never enough to eat. But Sammy had the worst of it; he was the oldest, and there was no one in the house to defend him. His father counted on the few pennies Sammy brought in from his papers and on days when business was bad Sammy was afraid to face him. Yesterday had been such a bad day and he lay awake all night thinking about what he could do to earn more money. From other boys he had heard that huckstering apples was a good job. You were sure of your wages and had plenty to eat besides. Sammy wondered why he had not thought of it before.

As soon as it grew light Sammy dressed and went out into the street. He did not have long to wait. From one of the avenues came a horse pulling a wagonful of apples. A man held the reins and walked alongside the horse. There was no one else with him. Sammy's heart stopped as he approached the man. But in a moment he was running upstairs to give his father the good news. The only thing the man had asked him was: "Can you holler loud?"

"Behave yourself, Sammy, and do what the man says!" His father's parting words rang in his ears as he ran out to start his day's work.

All day long he followed the horse and wagon and obeyed the boss's orders. Now, half-frozen, he was barely able to keep up. He walked silently, holding on to the wagon, his fingers numb.

"What happened to your tongue, Sammy?" exclaimed the boss angrily. "Let me hear you holler!"

"Hey! Apples!" Sammy screamed.

They approached a big apartment house. The boss nudged Sammy. "Go in there. But knock at each door. If you sell the apples, come right down for more. If not, go across the roof to the next place. But quick!"

Sammy ran into the house. The corridor was covered with

a carpet. He could feel the warmth coming from the steam radiators. He began knocking at doors. But no one needed apples. In one apartment a family sat around a table eating. Sammy could smell the food and his stomach tightened. From another apartment came a child's voice singing, a piano playing. A mother opened a door and sent her warmly-dressed Annie outdoors to play.

Sammy's heart ached with envy. He felt the tears coming to his eyes. In each apartment he saw light, warmth, comfort, love. But no one wanted his apples. He had already reached the top floor. He started up the steps leading to the roof. He could hear the rain beating on the tin and he stopped. The hallway was warm and dry. His weary, frozen limbs demanded rest.

"How will the boss know? He'll think I'm taking a little longer." He leaned wearily against a wall, then slid down to the floor. His head rested on the peck of apples held tightly in his lap. He felt himself falling asleep and started to get up in alarm but the rest of his movements were only in his dream . . .

Outside, the boss did not wait very long. The day's work was over anyway, it was time to send the boy home. True, the boy had the apples. But he owed him a quarter for the day's work and the apples were hardly worth that. Anyway, how much longer could he wait? He swore loudly and hoisted himself up on the wagon. "Let's go home!" The horse trotted off with renewed strength.

Sammy sat fast asleep in the topfloor hallway—and would have slept all night. But one of the tenants had left a line of wash hanging on the roof. She went to rescue it from the rain and stumbled over Sammy. Sammy jumped up more dead than alive and looked fearfully around him. A woman stood in front of him, her eyes blazing.

"What are you doing here? Get out!"

"Apples!" Sammy stammered. He darted wildly for the stairs. When he reached the street he was startled by the darkness. "Apples!" he cried once more, looking around for the wagon. But the street was empty.

He started running, hoping to catch up with the boss. But the streets were unfamiliar. He did not know where he was. With terror in his heart, he realized that he was lost. What difference did it make? What awaited him at home? But he ran and ran and ran. And the rain came down, harder and harder . . .

SHOLEM ASCH

SHOLEM ASCH

1880-1957

Almost from the very beginning, Sholem Asch's career was marked by feverishness and boundless productivity. The first collection of his stories in 1903 was favorably received by readers and critics. In 1904 DER FREIND, a literary periodical, began to print his novella, *Dos Shtetl*, an idyllic prose-poem of life in the small Jewish towns of Poland. His first play was presented the same year. In 1908 he traveled through Palestine and wrote of his impressions. In 1909 he visited the United States and on returning to Europe wrote a long short story and a play about Jewish life in America.

Never one to rest on his laurels, he was constantly seeking new themes. His translated works soon became popular in world literary circles. As the critic Sol Liptzin put it: "He was the first Yiddish writer of truly international vogue."

Sholem Asch's work, again almost from the beginning, has evoked controversy and contradictory opinion, creating both fanatical disciples and hostile critics. The critical literature about his work is voluminous. (During the last two decades of his life, he was in trouble with a segment of Jewish public opinion because of what his critics termed the "missionary" element in his novels about Christ and Christianity. Sholem Asch denied this, saying that he was trying only to show the common origins and the historical affinities of Judaism and Christianity.) His works span 4000 years of Jewish history and almost all of them are concerned with a search for the divine thread in Man, and with the key to Jewish survival.

When he came to know America better, a series of works based on Jewish life here came from his pen: *To America, Uncle Moses, The Mother, Chaim Lederer's Return, East River, Passage through the Night* — novels reflecting the profound changes taking place among American Jews. Many of these, as well as his Biblical and historical works, achieved considerable popularity in English translation.

A Union for Shabbos

by SHOLEM ASCH

Y OU THINK AMERICA is a *treyf* country? Not so. Whoever wants to, can be a Jew in America, and whoever is a *goy* from the old country, well, America won't help him either."

Thus spoke Nota Kukiriku the hide-stripper, as he tried to reassure Moishe-Aaron-Leyb Melamed, one day at Sabbath services, in the *Chevra Anshei Emess of Barasovitch* on Delancey Street.

Moishe-Aaron-Leyb Melamed had only just arrived from Barasovitch, bringing greetings from the old country, where he had been a devout *chassid* of the *Gerer Rebbe*. And he was terribly afraid of what might happen to his piety in America. But the troubles in the old country drove him out, so he had jeopardized his Jewishness and come to stay with his brother's two sons, of whom he had once been ashamed because they were not pious enough.

Pious they were not, but generous hearts they had. Moishe-Aaron-Leyb Melamed had only to hint that he needed their help and they immediately sent him a ship-ticket and some money to bring him to America. On his first Saturday here they didn't even go to work, for his sake; instead, they took him over to the synagogue where his *lantsleit* belonged, in order that he might meet some friends and that they might find him a job where he would not have to work on *Shabbos*.

When Moishe-Aaron-Leyb Melamed saw this Jewish *chevra* and heard the familiar sound of the *davnen* from Nota Kukiriku the hide-stripper, he felt somewhat reassured. Yes, it was the same Nota whom the *cheder*-boys had crowned with the name of Kukiriku because he crowed like a rooster when he *davned*. In the old country he had been a hide-stripper and had also had ambitions to lead the services in the *shul*, but they never even let him near the platform because he was a bit of an ignoramus, in fact, a real *grober yung*. But here in America he had become the "scholar" of the *chevra*! Still, he was a Jew. So Moishe-Aaron-Leyb felt reassured. The world was still a world, and everywhere there were Jews.

His *lantsleit* reassured him even further about his *Yiddishkeit;* that very Sunday morning they got him a job in a shirt factory in Brooklyn where only observant Jews worked. True, they earned very little, seven-eight dollars a week, but the boss himself was a pious Jew, a scholar, and at *mincha* time the whole shop stopped working and said the afternoon prayers. Of course, they had to make up for this *mincha* with a half-hour in the morning and a half-hour in the evening, but after all, the boss was not obligated to lose money just because he was a pious Jew.

"On the contrary," said the boss, "let everybody see that piety can succeed in America, too!" He was a stout little man with stubby, dirty fingers. "My competitors tell me that it

won't work, that my piety will ruin me and I'll be forced
to close my shop. Let's show them that devout Jews, too, can
turn out a good day's work, whether they *davn mincha* or
not."

The devout Jews really did want to show the other bosses
that it could be done. So they worked even harder. They
never wasted a minute by talking to each other. And when
Uncle Idel (the boss) saw his devout Jews bent over their
machines, working without a pause, he was most pleased.
He smiled and cracked his knuckles and yawned in satisfaction.

"And those wiseguys, those bums, want to start a union!
Without a union they won't work these days," he complained
to his workers, "but we don't need them here. We pray together in one *minyan*, at a real service, and what shop can
equal that? Let them answer that question, the union!"

His pious workers gratefully showered him with blessings
for his generosity. "God will reward you with good health
and long life!"

So Moishe-Aaron-Leyb Melamed, who had never held a
needle in his hand and who, as his wife said, "couldn't even
tie a knot in a cat's tail," learned the trade. "In America
you learn everything!" And with the same diligence he had
displayed in studying the Talmud he now worked on wom-
en's shirtwaists. At first he had felt embarrassed. A Jew like
Moishe-Aaron-Leyb Melamed, with a head full of *Rashi*
and *Tosefess*, with the sayings of the sages—and here they
wanted him to make blouses! Woman's work. So he used
to sit over a shirtwaist and think of a *Mishna*, or of an *agada*
from the *gemora*, or a law from the *Shulchan Aruch*, and
he would study it over in his head. But he soon grew accustomed to his new work. The *mishnas* and *agadas* flew out
of his head and disappeared and all that was left was shirts
. . . shirts . . . shirts . . .

But still, he did not completely give up what was his. He got up at four in the morning, studied a chapter of *mishna*, recited his psalms, said the morning prayers, and then went off to work. At night, he fell like a rock onto his bed, mumbling the *krishma* in a half-sleep, thankful that his boss at least allowed his workers to *davn mincha* in a *minyan*. At least one prayer a day said with a congregation, at least one *kedusha*—thank God for that!

But soon it happened as the prophet had foretold; "Israel grew fat and sinned." The pious boss began to trim his beard; the longer his devout Jews worked for him, the shorter grew his beard and his coat. "He's trying to become a *Daitch!*" But others said, "He's doing it for business." Whatever the reason, he no longer joined his workers in the *mincha* prayers. "The poor man is rushed, he has no time!"

One morning the men came to work and found several girls sitting at the machines. Naturally, they refused to sit down together with the females and asked to be placed apart from them. For a while this was arranged. But after a few weeks the boss decided that he was not running a synagogue, where the men and women had to sit separately. The pious Jews sighed deeply but said nothing.

Then one afternoon when they rose from their machines to *davn mincha*, as had become their habit, the boss came out and explained coldly that his shop was not a prayer-house. Whoever wanted to *davn* could do so at home. Here you had to work.

"But Reb Idel, how can you say that? You're a synagogue Jew yourself!"

"Whether I am or not is none of your business! I pay you for working, not praying!"

But they paid no attention to him. Every day when *mincha* time came around, one of the men would rise in his corner and sing out *Ashrei Yoshvei Veysecho,* and from all corners of the shop came a chorus of *Ashrei's*, and there was no stopping them. In vain the boss yelled, threatened, screamed. The men continued their prayers, finished them, and *then* went back to work.

But the shop kept growing bigger and bigger. More and more young women came to work there. And the longer they all worked the fatter grew the boss's belly and the brighter his eyes sparkled.

Finally, one day, he announced to his workers that since he had remodeled his shop and modernized it, his employees would now be required to work on Saturdays and rest on Sundays. When the pious Jews heard this they felt as though the earth were opening up beneath them. But Moishe-Aaron-Leyb Melamed resolved to risk his life for God and cried out, like Judah to his brother Joseph:

"Your honor the boss! And even if you beat us with iron whips as did Nevuzaradan the Wicked, do you think you will ever force us to desecrate the holy Sabbath, God forbid?"

"You don't have to! Whoever doesn't like it can get out of here! And you, insolent tongue who talks back to his boss, will be the first to get out!"

At this point Moishe-Aaron-Leyb Melamed remembered his two nephews with the generous hearts. "Come with me, brothers!" he said to his fellow workers, "I have an idea!" And they all followed him out of the shop.

That same evening, the pious Jews from Uncle Idel's shop held their first strike meeting. Moishe-Aaron's two nephews explained about unions. The leaders of the union made speeches. But the speech which made the deepest impression on the strikers was the one delivered by Moishe-Aaron-Leyb Melamed himself.

"Gentlemen! And there has arisen a Haman, wickeder than the wicked, who wants to force Jews to desecrate the Sabbath, and like Pharaoh he compels us with iron whips to work like slaves at hard labor. Jews! Let us give our lives for God and let us strike to safeguard the Torah and its commandments. Whoever follows us will receive the blessings of the Torah. And upon the Wicked will fall all the curses of Scriptures. Amen. Selah. Jews, be strong! Whoever is for God let him follow me!"

After two weeks of a bitter strike in which the pious Jews displayed a marked ability to fight, they returned to the shop with "timbrels and dancing." They had won all their demands. And the first demand was: The Sabbath will be observed and time for *mincha* will be allowed. Along with this went a raise in pay, and union hours.

Now they *davn mincha* not in haste, as before, but with dignity and solemnity. And when the boss is in the shop, they honor him with *kedusha*. "It's *his* money, let him get some enjoyment out of it!" the men smile into their beards.

And Moishe-Aaron-Leyb Melamed has become the most devoted union man. *"Oova!"* he says. "It's a great Improver of the World, the union. Without it, Jews would be at everybody's mercy, God forbid . . ."

First Day in School

by SHOLEM ASCH

(Chapter from a novella, To America. Yosele has come to America two years after the rest of the family.)

DURING THE TWO YEARS he had not seen Beryl and Chaim they had changed completely. He was almost afraid of them. Were these really his brothers? No, it was not possible! Their faces were not Jewish faces. They went around all day bareheaded. Their jackets were cut short. They spoke to each other in a tongue he did not understand. They sat down to meals without washing their hands or saying the accompanying blessing—and were not even afraid to do this in front of Father.

Nor were they the only ones who had changed. Rocheleh, his sister, dressed like a rich lady and was out of the house all day. Mama was different, too. She saw Beryl and Chaim chop wood on the Sabbath and light the fire, and did not rebuke them or even look at them disapprovingly. And

Father, costumed in a peculiar-looking short coat, would come home from work at night, bury his head in his newspaper, and barely exchange a word with anyone.

Yosele had been here two weeks already and nobody had suggested taking him to a *cheder*. There had been some talk about enrolling him in the school which Beryl and Chaim attended. But in the meantime, he stayed in the house with Mama, because he was afraid to go down into the street. No matter how hard his brothers tried to persuade him, he refused to go down into the street. He was afraid of the strangeness, the noise. So he dawdled around the house, but could not become accustomed to that either. Everything was strange—the house, his brothers, even his mother. She dressed differently, spoke differently.

Yosele felt lost.

Once, to make himself feel better, he took the *gemora* out of the bookcase and sat down to study. Mama stood in a corner and watched him and wept for joy. But before long, his brothers stormed into the house, made fun of him, and tried to drag him away from the book. Through the open doors and windows he could hear the sounds of the street —yelling, screeching, clattering. The tones of a hurdy-gurdy finally enticed him down into the street. So many children there! The man at the hurdy-gurdy turned a handle. Children danced in time to the music. Others were gathering up scraps of paper from the gutters to start a bonfire. Boys were playing ball, laughing and shouting and calling him to join the game.

But he was afraid and stayed a safe distance away. His brothers kept pulling at him, but he was afraid. Afraid of the strange children. Afraid of the noise. He ran back into the house and hid in a corner. Mama took him by the hand and led him down into the street again. She nudged him toward a group of boys.

"Go ahead, Yosele, play with the children!"

But Yosele was afraid, and ran back into the house again. He sat down with his *gemora,* poring over it like a scholar lost in thought.

Sometimes he would feel unbearably homesick, even though he knew that the old country was no longer his home; that his home was here where his mother and father were. But this was not the home he yearned for. Somewhere there was a home where Father had once sat chanting from the Talmud. Somewhere there was a home where Mama had stood before the Sabbath candles, blessing them and praying for a good week.

But sometimes, even now, when his father was at home in the evenings, and Yosele would take the *gemora* out of the bookcase, and Father would sit down with him to study a passage, and he heard the familiar chant, it would seem to him that he was back in the old home, that he had found something he had lost, and then both of them, father and son, would again feel close to each other. As time went on, you could find them more and more often sitting together over the *gemora* in their kitchen in the middle of the big, bustling city of New York.

Finally the day arrived when Yosele was to be enrolled in public school. Several times a man had come asking about him. So on this day Mama took him by one hand and Beryl by the other and they marched Yosele off to school.

At first, Yosele was frightened by the massive building. But when he saw how much at home his brother was, how cordially everyone greeted him, he felt somewhat more at ease. Beryl led them into the office, where they asked his mother a lot of questions. It took a while before his mother was able to persuade Yosele to remove his hat. He marveled at his brother Beryl, talking so freely with the tall, official-looking gentleman behind the desk.

Then Beryl took Yosele by the hand again and led him

into a huge room. Yosele objected all along the way, pleading with his mother to come into the room with him. But she refused. "Go along, son, go along. There's nothing to be afraid of. Look, Beryl is going in there, too!"

But when Yosele entered that room he was completely overwhelmed. Never before had he seen anything like it. An enormous room, bigger than a synagogue, the children sitting on chairs lined up across the entire length of the room. He hardly noticed that someone had sat him down on one of the chairs. He stared at the platform in front, filled with elegant lords and ladies. He heard the sounds of an organ, which a Jew must not listen to because there had once been such an instrument in the Holy Temple in Jerusalem.

Its tones were so solemn, and thundered so powerfully inside that spacious room, that Yosele was frightened and tears came to his eyes. Yet all the children were singing a song with such a beautiful, sweet melody, that it tugged at his heart. Surely this is how it must have been in the Holy Temple. And here he was, sitting and listening to it without a hat on his head . . .

Then the singing stopped and the children got up noisily out of their seats and moved off in various directions. Again he watched in amazement as Beryl greeted one of the ladies and spoke with her easily and smiled at her happily—as though she were one of the family! And now Beryl and the lady were coming toward him and she was smiling at him and saying words which he did not begin to understand. Yosele blushed and lowered his head and did not look at her. But she tucked her finger under his chin and raised his head and smiled at him and patted him gently on the head and he could feel the redness covering his face.

He looked frantically around for Beryl as she led him out of the hall. But his brother had disappeared, and the lady was guiding him across a wide corridor and up a lot of stairs and smiling at him and talking to him and pointing now at one thing and now at another. Yosele did not know what she meant. Yosele did not comprehend at all what was going on around him. It was some kind of dream and he could not recall how he came to be in it.

At the top of the stairs, the lady took him into another big room, although this one was not as big as the first. But it was full of children and as soon as they saw him they all began to laugh. It was a joyful laughter. They were not mocking him, only staring at him with friendly curiosity. The lady sat him down behind a desk and placed a sheet of paper before him. She pointed to a picture on the wall at the front of the room, handed him a pencil, pointed to the paper, then to the picture again, and left him. He was aware of her only vaguely as she moved among the other children.

Yosele sat stiffly with the pencil in his hand. After a little while he was able to look around him more calmly. The sun was shining in through the large, open windows, the same sun which used to shine in through the one window of Reb Yitzhok Yudl's *cheder*. But there it had been only a *piece* of the sun. Here it was the *whole* sun. Everything here was bigger.

There, in the *cheder*, his friend Moishele had sat next to him, and across from him Shloimele, the cantor's son. The *gemoras* had lain open before them on the long wooden table, and all the boys had chanted at the top of their voices, and the *rebbe* had moved slowly around the table with the cat-o-nine-tails in his hand, making sure that no one looked away from the book. A boy had only to look away for a second and whish! the cat-o-nine-tails whistled past his nose. The boys there knew the meaning of "the yoke of the Torah."

But here in America he was handed a sheet of paper and a pencil and told to look at the wall and draw pictures! And girls sat in the same room with boys and the children laughed

and played with the lady and everyone chattered at the same
time . . .

As he looked out at the sun he felt his heart break with
longing for Reb Yitzhok Yudl's *cheder*. How he wanted to
see Moishele and Shloimele again! How he wanted to chant
the *gemora* with them at the top of his voice! How he wanted
to display his knowledge of the Commentaries! But how far
ahead of him his friends must be by now! Surely they must be
starting a new Book of the Talmud by this time. And here he
was, drawing pictures . . .

What was he doing here anyway? How had he gotten here?
Where was he and what kind of place was it? He felt the
tears coming to his eyes, but he was ashamed to cry in front
of all the children. He sat silently in a strange, unimagined
world, as though all of this were taking place in a dream.

Someone spoke to him. He looked around him. The boy
sitting alongside him, a boy with unruly hair and fierce
eyes, was asking him something in a language Yosele did not
understand—and even the children around him did not
understand it either. (This was an Italian boy from Sicily
who, like Yosele, had just been tossed into the great American
melting-pot—the public school—and he had been sitting here
three days without understanding a word anyone was saying.)
Yosele moved fearfully away, but the boy began to pummel
him. Exasperated by his helplessness in these unfamiliar surroundings, he struck out blindly at the nearest person he
could reach.

The teacher perceived immediately what was wrong.
Calmly she quieted the Sicilian boy and moved Yosele to
another desk. And as she did so, she looked at Yosele af-
fectionately, patted his head, and said to him in Yiddish:

"*Hub kein moireh nisht* . . . don't be afraid . . ."

Yosele looked up at her in astonishment. A sense of profound understanding came over him in a rush. She had

spoken to him in Yiddish! The teacher must be just as home-sick as he was! It *must* be so, else why would she have so much love and compassion in her eyes? The teacher was someone he could trust . . .

But soon the dream sensation returned and enveloped him. And later, when his brother Beryl took him by the hand and dragged him to a little park, he felt lost again and begged Beryl to take him home.

At home, Yosele sat down in a corner and refused to move from there. His mother pleaded with him, but he would not listen. From the street came the sounds of children at play and the merry tunes of the hurdy-gurdy.

"Tell me what happened today at school," his mother begged.

But Yosele was silent.

In the evening, when his father returned from work and the family had finished their supper, Yosele took the *gemora* out of the bookcase and looked pleadingly at his father. They sat down to study, chanting the ancient words in unison. But they did not get very far. Yosele's chant was suddenly broken by sobs. His father's eyes filled with tears and he began to pace across the room, back and forth, back and forth, chewing the corners of his beard . . .

ABRAHAM REISIN

ABRAHAM REISIN

1875-1953

Abraham Reisin won immediate recognition among Yiddish readers as a sensitive poet when his first poems were published in the United States. (He was then living in Europe and had shown one of his poems to Sholem Aleichem, who enthusiastically submitted it to a Yiddish newspaper in Philadelphia.) Reisin, after a few visits, settled in the United States in 1914. In 1917 an edition of his collected poems and stories was published in eleven volumes. His verse is musical, direct and uncomplicated, but is imbued with a lyric emotion which aptly expressed his own changing mood and the quiet joys and sorrows of his many readers.

Reisin was also a master of the short sketch—the *skitze*—and wrote hundreds of deceptively simple pictures of ordinary people and their everyday problems. Taken together, however, his little sketches add up to much more than "the sum of the parts." They make up a large canvas of the Jewish life of the time, both in Europe and America.

It is no exaggeration to say that Reisin developed a perfect art form. A superfluous word, either in his poems or in his stories, is a rarity. His mark is the spare stroke. And he was able to ensnare the most complicated ideas in this simple form. Essential to the success of this process was, of course, his ability to select the proper episode and the right moment.

"Reisin does not moralize, nor does he employ any subtle psychological analysis to uncover the souls of his characters. He merely relates incidents and episodes, but these episodes speak for themselves, and like a lightning-flash, illuminate the dark horizon of the life of these characters." (Meyer Waxman, *History of Jewish Literature, Vol. 4*)

About the style and purpose of his writing, Reisin himself said: "Certainly my stories are written on the basis of reality. But this is the only kind of writing that can add anything to what has already been said by somebody else . . . To make life more human, that is the highest end."

Chasing After Villa

by ABRAHAM REISIN

WHERE MY BENNY IS, you want to know? Thanks for asking. Although when you remind me of him, my heart breaks. Imagine—*my* Benny chasing after Villa! Which Villa? Don't you read the papers? Really? I mean Villa from Mexico, the one we have to capture "dead or alive." He's the one my Benny's running after . . .

Two years ago, Benny was working in a shop—when there was work, that is. Just as often, he wasn't working at all. So he got sick and tired of both things, working and loafing, because here in America neither condition is exactly a bed of roses. Working in a shop was too hard for him. Not because he didn't have the strength—it wasn't that at all. But he can't stand "walls," my Benny. That's what *he* complained about. And when he wasn't working, *I* complained—a healthy young man like him sitting on his father's neck!

So one fine morning he went and enlisted in the Army. There's America for you! Did you ever hear of such a thing back in that miserable old country—that a young fellow would *volunteer* for the army? There he would thank God if something was wrong with him—a whistling in his ears, or varicose veins, or a dozen missing teeth, or other such lucky defects which the authorities had so much respect for. My Benny, thank God, did not have any of these things wrong with him. The only fault he had was whistling. Not his ear, God forbid, but his mouth. Whenever he used to start whistling in the house, I was afraid all the spirits in all the forests would come running, as we used to believe in the old country.

So he went to enlist in the American army. But that's easier said than done. As hard as it was to get *out* of the army back home, that's how hard it is to get *into* the army here. Oh, they'll take you, allright, but first—first your father has to sign a paper.

He comes home one day, my Benny, sticks this paper under my nose and announces that whereas he hates to work in a shop and whereas I won't stand for his loafing, therefore he has made up his mind to join the army. And when he finishes his service in the army, God willing, he will get a job as a policeman on a horse.

Why on a horse, I asked him. Why not a policeman on foot who protects society with both feet on the ground? So Benny explained to me that he has long legs and because he has long legs he wants to join the cavalry and afterwards he can be a mounted policeman and protect society from a height.

Well, I liked it and I didn't like it. I didn't like it that my Benny, who in Russia would probably have been exempted because he is older than my youngest boy by about seven years, should turn out to be a soldier in America. True, he was volunteering, nobody was forcing him, but still, I'd rather he didn't. On the other hand, it wouldn't be so bad to have a son a policeman, especially on a horse. Because if he's on a horse, they won't put him somewhere on Hester Street, but on Fifth Avenue, where the automobiles run all, day and the millionaires go for a stroll.

I asked the lawyer from my *lantsmanshaft*: What kind of rights will I be entitled to if my son becomes a soldier? And the lawyer told me that in the first place, I would become "almost" a citizen. Which means that if I ever take a trip to Europe, the American government must let me back into this country. Or if I ever wanted to open a saloon, I could get a license easier than somebody else. I would become a sort of relative to Uncle Sam.

I kept changing my mind—yes, no, yes, no—until finally I signed the paper. Which meant that I agreed that my son Benny should be of service to the United States of America. The main thing that convinced me was that I would become a part-citizen, because to become a whole citizen is impossible for me. Not that I haven't been here long enough. I have. And I could have become a citizen three times over, if it wasn't for my mixed-up head. Who has a brain to learn all those things? Just because I have one free day in the week—sometimes Saturday and sometimes Sunday, depending on what shop you work in—should I break my head trying to learn new tricks—like what was the name of the 19th President of the United States?

Of course, if I had only known they would "assign" him to a place that's one jump away from Mexico, and that Pancho Villa would make a revolution and start up with America! That was something I didn't expect! Who can be smart enough to figure all that out in advance? To tell you the truth, I didn't even know that Mexico is a separate country and doesn't belong to our America.

So now things are not so pleasant. I'm sure my Benny is down there in Mexico chasing after Villa, because I haven't received a letter from him for a long time. Before, he used to write me every week and even send me a few dollars from his pay. He gets pretty good wages—15 dollars a month plus room and board. It wouldn't be such a bad job if it weren't for Villa.

One thing my heart tells me. If Villa lets himself be caught it will be my Benny who'll catch him. Benny is a boy who's afraid of nothing! I only hope he captures him alive, because after all, why spill human blood? I don't believe in wars. I ask you, who needs it and what kind of world has it become when even America couldn't manage to get out of this situation—this whatever it is—if it's not a war, it's a hunting expedition . . .

And who has to catch him, Villa I mean? Nobody but my Benny himself, who's been in this country only ten years! I don't say they forced him, you understand, but who knows, if he had had a steady job he might never have thought about the army and I would be able to sleep peacefully. But the way things are, every night I dream about my Benny chasing after him, Villa I mean, and Villa is nobody's fool —he keeps running away.

The other day I went to the movies and they showed a picture about Mexico and how our boys are running things down there. People sit in the movies and beam and applaud Bravo! Bravo! Maybe I'd be just as patriotic as they are if my Benny wasn't down there in the middle of it. But my hands refused to clap—they were too busy wiping the tears from my eyes. One of the soldiers on a horse looked just like my Benny—he was gazing at me sadly as though he regretted the whole thing. I wanted to get a better look but the picture changed to a ship with a big cannon. You should have heard the people cheer! What were they so happy about —that Uncle Sam has a cannon?

Never mind. When *their* sons have to go down there they won't be so tickled about cannons . . .

The Contribution

by ABRAHAM REISIN

OLLIE AND KATIE, both of them dark-haired, pretty and slender, accepted their new union assignment with deep satisfaction. It was not the first time they had done work of this kind. In the old country they had carried out many similar missions, except that there they had raised funds for the "Bund." Naturally, not everyone was supposed to know that they were collecting money for the Bund. They had acted under the guise of charity-collectors for needy Jews.

But here in America they could tell everyone freely and candidly the purpose of their collection. In fact, they didn't really have to *say* anything. Each of them wore a red ribbon across her chest, announcing in gold letters: FOR THE STRIKERS. And the same message was inscribed on the collection cans.

Their task was more pleasant than not. Thanks to the newspapers, the strike had become a much-talked about sensation. And only two days before, a thousand young women, strikers all, had marched down Broadway carrying red banners blazoning forth their demands. The march had made a favorable impression upon the bystanders. Young men with nothing else to do at the time had followed the march along the entire route with appreciative eyes. Other young men, who understood the importance of a strike, had joined the parade "to help the cause." (This did not prevent them, however, from taking advantage of the opportunity to make dates with the rank-and-file!) Even the "capitalist press" had given the demonstration a good deal of coverage.

The Socialist newspaper outdid itself, giving the march four full pages at the expense of some of its most popular daily features. The columns describing the march were full of bitter attacks against the owners of the shops where the girls worked. The reporter, a man not without talent, and with a passionate temperament, himself a former shop-worker, displayed a fierce hostility to employers as a class. He practically called for a social revolution, and similar ideals, which are so easy to write about when the ink is fresh and the paper is white and the pen is new and sharp . . .

Understandably, after such a demonstration and so much sympathetic newspaper coverage, Mollie and Katie found it extremely easy to collect funds. Of pennies there was no end —these little coins flew into the slot of the collection cans with magical speed. Even nickels were tossed at them willingly and joyfully. And in one cafe, a hangout for young writers and union leaders (who are always young), the two girls were practically showered with contributions. One writer, who had a reputation as something of a Don Juan, but who was really in love with the *poetry* of pretty girls, put in a whole quarter.

The largest contribution, however, was given to them near a subway station where they had stopped to catch the homeward-bound working-people. Out of the station strode a tall, solidly-built man with big shoulders and a massive head covered with a new hat. His coat was unbuttoned, revealing a heavy watch-chain across his vest. A gold stickpin shone in his silk necktie.

The two girls took one look at him, glanced at each other in a silent conference, and at the last moment, Mollie boldly but nervously touched his elbow.

"Something for the strikers, mister . . ." she murmured.

The man stopped, inspected her with an ambiguous smile, and asked what trade was on strike. She told him, and his smile became even more ambiguous.

"Yes, I've heard about it," he said amicably. "A hard trade to work in . . . the girls are right . . . What is it they want, exactly?"

Mollie and Katie, enraptured by the interest this fine gentleman was displaying in the troubles of their sisters, enlightened him volubly concerning the theory and practice of the strike. There seemed to be no limit to the interest and concern shown by this friend of labor. He was also very much interested in the question of strike tactics.

"Please, my dear children, how long do you think you'll stay out?"

"Until we win all our demands!" Mollie replied with fire in her eyes.

"Until we wear down the bosses!" Katie cried militantly.

"Right . . . right . . ." the man agreed. "They deserve it, those bosses. Tell me, children, do all the strikers feel this way? Everybody is one hundred percent for the strike?"

"Everybody!" Mollie assured him confidently.

"We're united! Solid as a wall!" echoed Katie, quoting from one of the strike songs.

The man smiled more broadly, wrinkled his brow and murmured: " Good . . . good . . . very good . . . outstanding . . ." He took his wallet out of his breast pocket, opened it, found a five-dollar bill, folded it neatly, and slipped it into the collection can. Then he tipped his hat, smiled again in a most friendly manner, and walked away.

"Who do you think he is?" Mollie gasped, her face beaming with surprise and achievement.

"Must be a worker who struck it rich," guessed Katie.

"A fine man . . ." said Mollie.

"A cultured man . . ." Katie seconded.

"Not bad looking, either," mused Mollie.

"Handsome, in fact," corrected Katie.

* * *

The handsome gentleman had by this time forgotten even what the two girls looked like. It was their words that intrigued him more. He turned into a side street and pondered what they had said. "Solid as a wall!"

Eventually he stopped at a modest-appearing home and rang the doorbell. A man opened the door cautiously before admitting him. A group of important-looking men sat around a table. It was obviously a meeting. The chairman at the head of the table greeted the new arrival:

"Well, Mr. Miller, what's the latest?"

"The latest is that I've just learned a lot from two pretty girls with collection cans. And it cost me five dollars to learn it." His eyes clouded over. "It's going to be a long, hard strike." He took a seat at the table. "Give me back my five dollars, Mr. Secretary. Charge it to Strike Expenses."

The Secretary of the Employers Association took a bill out of a cashbox, made an entry into a ledger, and repaid Mr. Miller his contribution.

Save Your Dimes

by ABRAHAM REISIN

FTER MANY WEEKS of unemployment, Rose and Bertha finally found work in a shirtwaist factory. The day they received their first pay they were so happy that walking home from work they stopped now and then to take the dollar bills out of the envelopes and count and recount them, almost embracing them as one does old friends whom one has not seen for a long, long time.

But in the middle of their merriment, Rose suddenly grew solemn. She stopped playing with her money. The smile disappeared from her lips, as she said seriously to her companion:

"What are we going to do about all our debts?"

Bertha's face grew serious, too, but only for a fleeting moment. She laughed. "Let's declare bankruptcy like the big businessmen do!"

"I'd like to see you tell that to the missus," Rose smiled despite her gloomy thoughts. "She'll toss us out into the street . . ."

"Ach, the missus, the missus!" Bertha echoed. "Let's move out in the middle of the night!"

In the course of their walk they had paused outside a stationery store. The window was inartistically strewn with all sorts of toys, school supplies, showcards. They stared into the window and continued their discussion about the disbursement of their "assets." A little showcard caught Rose's eye. SAVINGS BANK—$1.00.

"Look at that, Bertha," she murmured. "A bank. You can save up money in it . . ."

Bertha got the idea at once. She was enchanted by that bank. It was not a coincidence to be lightly disregarded. She pulled Rose into the store.

The storekeeper, a man in his early fifties, with a kind, fatherly expression on his face, got up from his chair and walked toward the candy case. By their happy mood he judged them to be candy customers. Rose's practical tone of voice soon showed him his error.

"I'd like to buy one of those banks," she said matter-of-factly.

"Me, too," said Bertha like a little girl.

The storekeeper's fatherly expression changed to one of pious satisfaction. His eyes shone and he placed his hands together.

"That's fine! Good! Very nice! Saving money is a worthwhile idea. Why waste your money on foolish things? Save up twenty dollars and you can put it to good use. Ay, *kinnder,* so many uses you can find for it!" And giving the two girls a friendly, almost grateful look, he reached up on a shelf, took down two dime banks and placed them on the counter before him.

Rose and Bertha examined the banks on all sides, and the storekeeper meanwhile delivered a lecture on how to operate them.

"For instance, let's say tonight you want to go to the moving-pictures. You stop and think—why throw out ten cents on such foolishness? Wouldn't it be better to throw the dime into this slot here? You understand? When you put the dime in there you know it's safe. You can't get it out again. It's like putting it into a grave. But don't be frightened, children. It won't die in there. When you put your money into that slot you'll hear a bell ring. Then you'll see the number 10 right here on this register. Tomorrow, you put in another dime. Another ten cents hidden away so you can't waste it. But the register here will now show 20 cents. And when you finally put 200 dimes into that grave, then all of them will come back to life. The bank will start ringing happily and this door here will open by itself and all the dimes will come flying out!"

"Two hundred dimes! All at once!" Bertha couldn't get over it.

"Not one of them will be missing!" the storekeeper assured her.

The two girls paid him for the banks, and with their heads full of pleasant fantasies of a rich future, they walked out of the store with the savings-banks firmly in their hands.

During the next two weeks Rose saved up 60 cents in her bank. Bertha's register showed only 40 cents, although Bertha was quite certain she would catch up with her friend. All she had to do was skip the movies once or twice, or the baked apple with cream which she loved to eat at Child's . . . What did she need the baked apple for anyway?

And it's possible that her bank would have caught up to Rose's had not something happened which had happened so often before. Their boss ran out of work. Rose and Bertha had to postpone indefinitely their idea of saving up twenty dollars.

Crestfallen and humiliated the two banks stood on their bureaus, the numbers 40 and 60 looking like brief inscriptions on humble gravestones.

One day, as they sat in their little room wondering how to pay the week's rent, Bertha suddenly stared at the two banks and burst out laughing.

"What's so funny all of a sudden?" Rose snapped testily. Lately her nerves were always on edge.

"I just remembered what he said—the man who sold us the banks. All the dimes will come back to life! That's very funny!" she giggled foolishly.

Soon Rose began to giggle, too, as she stared dolefully at the banks. "I don't believe in that any more—that people come back to life . . ."

Bertha was by nature more optimistic. She walked over to Rose's bank and looked seriously at the figure 60 standing so proudly inside the register. Despite the smile on her face, her tone was solemn.

"What do we need two of these for?" she said to Rose. "Let's open one of them up and resurrect our old friends!"

Rose looked at her with a puzzled expression. "But how? It won't open till it has 200 dimes . . ."

"Who said so? There aren't that many dimes in the whole world. We ought to get those six dimes out of their grave and go eat supper."

"But how?" Rose had already come to the conclusion that it would be a good idea.

"We'll break it open," said Bertha flatly.

"Are you crazy?"

"No. I'm hungry!"

"Well, all right. Let's see you do it . . ."

"Don't worry. I'll do it. Right now I could break open a real bank-building!"

Bertha attacked the bank with every weapon she could find in the room—knives, scissors, spoons, shoes—but it held fast. It absolutely refused to surrender its six victims. Bertha grew angrier and angrier. She snatched up the bank and began to beat it on the floor and against the wall. The room seemed to fill with a struggle between life and death.

The missus burst into the room. "What's going on here!"

"I'm fixing my trunk," Bertha grimaced sheepishly.

The missus shrugged her shoulders suspiciously and left. Bertha resumed her offensive. She smashed the bank on all sides until it grew red with blood . . .

"Bertha! You've cut your fingers!" cried Rose.

"So what? Those dimes have our blood in them, too!"

Rose felt tears coming to her eyes, but she knew she now had to help her courageous friend in her war against the bank. She giggled as they both pulled at it violently. Soon the battle was over. The savings-bank submitted and split in two.

A thing of magic lay exposed to their marveling eyes. Inside the metal covering, a complicated mechanism wrapped in paper numbers still tried valiantly to conceal the silver dimes . . .

They picked out the coins carefully one at a time as they had both done so often in their dreams. With the dimes in their hands they were cheerful again as they went out to buy their supper.

The broken savings-bank lay helpless on the floor like a vandalized grave. And the second bank stood on a bureau with the number 40 staring fearfully out at the world, knowing full well it was destined for the same fate as its brother on the floor . . .

The Trial

by ABRAHAM REISIN

ACK IN MY *shtetl* I was always scared to death of courts. "Nobody knows the laws," says the Prophet. And thank God—I never had to stand trial for anything. Well, that's not exactly true. Once, during the cholera epidemic—God forbid it should ever happen here—the authorities got very strict about "sanitation" and the police wanted to fine me for a little bit of garbage which I dumped outside my door. I was supposed to stand trial, but I slipped a flunkey a ruble and that was the end of it.

Here in America, I thought, I would certainly never have to worry about anything like that. It's a democratic country and nobody makes false charges; about sanitation they don't worry too much on my street; special Jewish taxes you don't have to pay; identity cards are not required—a free country, do what you like. But it turns out that even here in this free country I had to stand trial, God protect me! Blood and cash it cost me!

And who do you think put me on trial? Gentiles? Yankees? Americans? Not at all! Jews did it. My own brothers.

In the old country I was a plain tailor. I struggled for a living. Whatever people brought me, I fixed—a lady's dress, a peasant's coat, a boy's pants, anything. I was no specialist, in other words. But here in this country they don't allow it. Here, everybody has his own craft. And since I have quick hands, they told me I would do better at "cloaks," that is, women's coats. So the moment I landed in this country I became a "cloak-maker."

Well, before the big strike, you know how it was—real freedom with a capital F. You want to work piecework, work piecework. You want to work by the week, work by the week. You want to work till three in the morning, go ahead and more power to you! Nobody could tell you what to do. So there were times when I made a nice pay, almost forty dollars in one week. You know what that means? True, it was hard work. Some nights I didn't even go home to sleep—just laid down for a couple of hours in the shop. Sometimes I didn't take my clothes off for two-three days at a time. So what of it? Whose business is it? As long as I have the strength and there's all day Saturday to sleep. Saturday I never work, no sir! Not that I go to the synagogue—maybe I should, but I don't.

But somebody got the idea that this wasn't fair. One man earns forty dollars a week and twenty men are out of work . . .

Tell me yourself. Hasn't it always been that way? Whoever is ambitious, has quick hands and isn't lazy, makes more money. Those who have no work? I'm sorry for them. But is it my fault? Don't I have to worry about myself, too?

Believe me, forty dollars a week wasn't such a fortune for me. I brought with me a wife and four kids, and here we had three more, God bless them all. So what if I save a few dollars in the bank for a rainy day?

Anyway, came the big strike . . .

You don't have to tell me that a strike is a serious matter. Workingmen have to improve their conditions. It's not a sin. But I'm a father of seven children and I've been working for the same boss quite a few years and I have nothing against him, he's treated me fair and square. Matter of fact, he's my *lantsman*. Let the others strike. I won't make any fuss and I'll keep on working.

But it turns out that in this country that's one of the worst crimes. I don't mean in the eyes of the government. In fact, the government approves of it. But the workers call you a "scab."And a scab is like a Jew who's been excommunicated.

What could I do? I had to put down my tools with the rest of them. Believe me, it was really hard for me to turn on my boss this way. He gave me a look that broke my heart. You work for a man for five years, he gives you your pay every single week without fail, he treats you right, and suddenly you turn around and tell him: "No more work!"

But it was out of my hands. When the Union says "do something," you have to do it! That Union! It's a real government, with officials, delegates, organizers, secretaries—all they need is uniforms and brass buttons!

Twelve weeks that strike lasted! Lucky for me I had saved a few dollars. True, they paid us a little "strike benefits" during the first few weeks. But how far could that go? They ran out of money—and no wonder! More than 50,000 cloakmakers were out on strike! Where could the Union get that much money?

Twelve weeks work went down the drain. You think I

rested those twelve weeks? Not on your life! Every night I had to go to a meeting where the speakers made long speeches about the power of the workers and how the bosses had been sucking our blood, and how we must put a stop to it. As soon as one speaker finished, another one started all over again with the same words, so the workers would understand the message.

I won't deny it. During those three months I got a little education. I learned a lot of new English words, because the speakers, who had all been in this country a few years, mixed a lot of English into their Yiddish, but I could understand them fine. Sometimes they even convinced me. I would see that it really was not right that the boss should make so much money and the worker so little. They won me over completely to their side. After everything is said and done—I felt—all these speakers are really our friends, they really care what happens to us.

There was only one thing I could never agree to—that I should become an enemy of my boss. By nature I am very respectful of rich people. I could never imagine myself a person of importance, me, a plain, ordinary workingman. Who was I to compare myself to my boss, a man who handles thousands of dollars every day in the week?

And the Union went and passed a rule that workers are not permitted to hold any private conversations with the boss. Finish your nine hours work and go home!

So when the strike was settled, it was a real shame for the bosses. Not that they made less money. It wasn't that. It was just that they were no longer bosses. They couldn't fire a worker or hire another one. Whatever they wanted to do they had to ask the Union first. You understand? What good was all their money when their word carried no weight? Because, just between us, why does a man want to get rich in the first place? I'll tell you why. So people will respect him, so people will know who he is, that his word is law, that his opinion must be listened to. But when a boss has a hundred men working for him and has no say about what they do, what good is his money?

That's why I felt sorry for the bosses. Not all of them, of course. It's not my business. Just my *own* boss. First of all, as I told you, he was my *lantsman*. Secondly, he was a man who loved *kovid*—a little "honor." So why shouldn't I show him respect? At least, as much as was due him. . . .

And that's where my troubles began. I wasn't worried about not being able to work as many hours as before the strike. You want me to work only nine hours, OK. Let all the cloakmakers have work—maybe it's not such a bad idea. But why should it bother you if I'm friendly with the boss? Or if I come in to work before anybody else and *shmuess* with him a little bit? Or stay after work a half-hour and listen to his complaints. Sometimes he's right, you know. When he starts complaining about the Union, my heart breaks.

You take a king and deprive him of his crown, his power, his army. You tell him: "Keep your gold and your treasures, we won't touch it. But don't interfere in the government!" Exactly as it is happening now with the Persian Shah and the Portuguese King and the Turkish Sultan, like the papers write.

I tried to console him. A few times, when there was a special rush job to be finished, I stayed overtime when all the others had gone home. I didn't have the heart to turn him down. So I put in a little overtime and helped him out. Until one of the men found out about it.

"What kind of business do you have with the boss?" a young shnook asked me one morning. In the good old days I wouldn't even have bothered answering him. But now I wanted to get something off my chest.

"Who should I have business with—you? You're not even dry behind the ears yet!"

I heard a buzz travel round the shop. The foreman, though, was on my side. The strike had taken *his* rights away, too. But he couldn't help me now. All he could do was wink at me to give me courage.

After work, all the cloakmakers put on their coats to leave. But they didn't leave. They seemed to be waiting for something.

"Well, mister, why don't you go home?" the same young shnook asked me.

"I've got time," I said. "I'm in no hurry!" I was starting to get really mad. After a few minutes they left. I won my point and stayed and told the boss what I thought of them.

The next morning I found a "summons" from the Union on my machine. Come to a hearing. I read it through carefully and thought to myself: "After all, they're not *goyim*, they're Jews." And I didn't go.

About a week later, two delegates came into the shop and marched straight over to my machine: "Put on your coat and come along with us!"

The boss tried to stop them. 'What do you have against this man?"

"Everything will be brought out at the trial!" That was all they would say.

Well, what should I tell you? It was a real trial, like in Russia, with a presiding judge and sworn witnesses and a prosecutor and all the rest of it. Except for the defense attorney. I didn't have one.

The sentence was 75 dollars fine and transfer to another shop. Which meant simply: "Out, brother!"

The money didn't bother me so much. It was the transfer.

True, the shop where I now work is much bigger, much lighter, much airier, and it's on the first floor near a window.

In case of fire, God forbid, I could jump right out. But it's
not too pleasant for me. For one thing, the other cloakmakers
look at me like I was a criminal. They don't take their eyes
off me. I'm "under surveillance" so I won't talk with the boss.

They don't understand, these guys, that the boss—my new
boss—doesn't even know I exist. For another thing, he's a
German Yahudi and it's beneath him to talk to me in the first
place. They don't understand that. So all they do is watch
me. Not that it scares me. Once a week I manage to go up
to visit with my old boss. I pour my heart out to him. He
consoles *me* and I console *him*.

And we hope that sooner or later the Union will grant us
both a pardon . . .

JOSEPH OPATOSHU

JOSEPH OPATOSHU

1886-1954

Opatoshu made his home in the United States from the age of 21 until his death, and very quickly developed a feeling for the American environment, but he was equally at home in the woods, fields and cities of his native Poland. His major work, "*In Polish Woods*," is the story of a Jewish family, told against the background of the declining Chasidic movement. He attempted, too, in several works, to recreate certain Jewish historical periods—as did Sholem Asch—and in preparation made minute studies of Jewish life during those periods.

Jewish historians, he said, "have omitted the six days of the week and given us only the Shabbos and the Kiddush ha-Shem. It was this omission that drove me to write historical novels, to recreate the everyday life not only of the ordinary man of Rabbi Akiba's time, but also of Rabbi Akiba and his students."

When Opatoshu came to the United States in 1907 he worked in various shops, for a while sold newspapers, and at night studied engineering at Cooper Union. (He received an engineering degree, but never practiced the profession.)

He was one of the few Yiddish writers who paid special attention to the Jewish underworld, both in the old country and here in the United States. In many of his short stories he depicted the seamier side of the Jewish East Side—the life of its inhabitants who had become utterly devoid of the traditional Jewish values.

Opatoshu used a quick, vigorous prose in his shorter stories and sketches, and as he himself said, this was a consciously-developed style. "My work for the daily newspaper requires short stories. This has brought me to a special brevity in writing. I tried to add to the short story (which had already acquired a set pattern) a new form, a new character. I strive to bring out a maximum with a minimum of words, to present a segment of life with a minimum of description. I strive to give a story in *action*, not only in invented detail . . . I may not always succeed, but that is my intent."

Poker Game
In A Synagogue

by Joseph Opatoshu

THE SYNAGOGUE *"Shaarit Yisroel"* was on the verge of bankruptcy. The rabbi had not been paid for six months; the cantor, for a year; and nobody even worried about the *shammos.* Taxes, interest on the first mortgage, interest on the second mortgage, everything was overdue; everybody was clamoring for their money, threatening to "attach" the property. And the Depression had been raging for three years, getting into everyone's marrow. Some of the well-to-do members of the congregation had lost their money, some had left the neighborhood, and the rest had grown so cautious with their pocketbooks that nobody could get a penny out of them. The poor people—workingmen, tradesmen, old retired men and women living with their children—these became the donors who maintained the synagogue.

The few tradesmen, the few workingmen, and especially the older people who already had one foot in the next world, all of them swore to stay with the synagogue and for no price to relinquish it to the Negro population now streaming into the neighborhood. The Jewish population was growing sparser and sparser. The Jews were moving deeper and deeper into the Bronx, all the way to 240th Street. Where the Jews moved out, the Negroes moved in. They came from the neighboring streets and avenues, many of them unemployed and hungry. The men—shoe-shiners and window-cleaners. The women—domestics, maids, office-cleaners . . .

Soon they wanted to buy the synagogue building. They argued—if it's good enough for the Children of Israel it's good enough for us. But the tradesmen-workingmen's congregation would not hear of it. They taxed themselves, they went begging from door to door, they organized bridge-parties, anything to save the *shul*.

It was a quiet afternoon. In the small foyer of the synagogue building, six people—four men and two women—sat playing poker. Part of the winnings would go to pay a cantor for the High Holidays. The door leading from the foyer to the synagogue was locked. At the east end of the foyer stood a reader's stand, where on weekdays a *minyan* came in of an afternoon for *mincha* or *maariv*. Two *yortseit* candles flickered on the stand.

The card-players sat around a long, unpainted table, their faces wan and slack. Through the open windows oozed the August heat, breathing fire. The four men had thrown off their coats and vests. One of them had even taken off his hat and sat bare-headed in the foyer of the *shul*. The women— two store-keepers who had left their husbands to tend the business and had come hurrying to the *shul* as one hurries to perform an act of mercy— sat with the cards in their hands and gasped in the heat.

The players hardly spoke. They snuffled the cards skillfully and dealt them out; the chips tinkled on the long, wooden table like little bones. One of the women looked conspiratorially into her cards out of a corner of her eye. Her expression did not change. Nonchalantly she said:

"Twenty cents and double it."

"Thirty more!" another player said as he tossed in three chips.

"Forty!"

"Fifty!"

The chips tinkled, placed themselves in a heap—click-clack, click-clack. The players forgot that the winnings were to pay a cantor. The cards sucked them further and further into the game. The calm, indifferent storekeeper kept on buying chips, kept on taking change out of her linen purse. And when an hour had passed and she had not stopped losing, her calmness was a little shaken.

"I have no luck with cards . . ."

A herring-dealer, in a white coat spotted with fish-scales, was in the middle of a winning streak. He arranged his chips in stacks of ten, a dollar a stack, and counted aloud—three dollars, five dollars, seven dollars, eleven dollars. The eleven dollars he had won rose in the air and wafted themselves before his face like a fan. He felt good, the herring-dealer, and when he heard the lady storekeeper say with a sigh, "I have no luck with cards," he quipped:

"And how about with love?"

"That's *my* affair!"

"And in *mitzvas?*"

"When it comes to that," she said as she won her first pot and spit three times for luck, "I have enough *mitzvas* to sell you some of mine cheap!"

A peddler with a basket of stockings wandered into the synagogue. He looked at the card-players with obvious disapproval. He could see there would be no *minyan* here today. Slowly he walked to the reading-stand and began his prayers. When he finished he turned toward the card-players with a pained expression on his face, as though he wanted to say something. But he only sighed deeply. Then he recited the *kaddish*, picked up his basket of stockings and on his way out, purely from force of habit, he murmured to the players: "Six cents a pair, two pair for ten . . ."

No one took notice of him, or even heard what he said. Ten dollars lay in the pot. The game was getting hot, the stakes risky. From a ten-cent "high" they had gone up to twenty-five. The men had taken off their hats and were swaying over their cards as Talmud-students do over their page of *gemora*. The herring-dealer chanted:

"Another pot like this and we'll have enough for the *chazzan!*"

"Yes, for the *chazzan,*" another chimed in as he studied his "hand" and the herring-dealers's expression. (If he's raising so high he's either bluffing or he's got a straight.)

A boy of about fifteen came into the foyer from the street. He looked at the players and his pale, emaciated face blushed and paled again. He held out his hands complainingly:

"I have to say *kaddish!*"

"Who's stopping you?"

"How can I *davn* when you're sitting there bareheaded?"

"Yes, you'd better put your hats on," the woman advised. "It's not so terrible, you won't melt!"

The boy stared at the card-players with so much hostility and disgust that they felt impelled to defend themselves.

"He must think we do nothing all day but play cards . . ."

The boy went to the reading-desk and waited a moment for the players to quiet down. But the chips continued to clink. The words "straight . . . pass . . . raise" forced their way into the boy's prayer. Suddenly he backed away from the reading-stand and rushed to the table with such violence that the players covered their chips protectively. His voice rose to a furious scream.

"Stop clinking your chips! Stop playing cards! My father died this week and I want to say *kaddish!*"

"The card game is for the *shul,*" one of the men said sheepishly. "If we don't play cards, you won't have any place to say *kaddish . . .*"

The boy's tone softened. "Can't you wait until I finish? Just out of respect . . ."

"Go ahead, son, go say *kaddish,*" one of the women said. She stood up and motioned to the others to do the same.

The men—their hats on the back of their heads and the cards in their hands—stood up meekly and remained standing, waiting for the boy to finish the *kaddish,* so they could respond "Amen."

Family Pride

by JOSEPH OPATOSHU

ALMAN PUT THE telephone-receiver to his ear and listened. When he heard the girl's voice: "Ace Mattress Company" his own voice trembled.

"Please connect me with Mister Dave Fagin."

"Who's calling, please?"

"Mister Fagin's cousin."

There was a moment's silence. A stillness which makes you hold your breath. Then the girl's voice came on again.

"Mister Fagin is not here now."

During the next week Zalman called the mattress factory three-four times a day and each time his cousin was "not in". Each time the same girl, the same voice, the same questions, as though on the other end of the telephone sat not a human being but a machine. After each call Zalman cursed, and prayed that he should never need to have any dealings with his cousin. He was certain that Dave did not want to see him; that he was annoyed with his needy cousin for pestering him. And the longer the manufacturer avoided him the stronger grew Zalman's obstinacy. He determined to wait for Fagin in the street outside the factory; he began to feel that not only he—Zalman—but all workers had a share in Dave's wealth.

During the twelve years Zalman had been in New York he met his rich cousin only at family weddings and funerals. And because Fagin, the rich employer, acted so high and mighty, Zalman, the worker, acted even more so, just to show that as far as he was concerned the rich manufacturer could go to hell. And the two cousins would probably have lived out their days this way were it not for the Depression. Zalman's last dollar, the last piece of his wife's jewelry, had been spent or pawned. Eight months of unemployment had taken their toll. His proud head began to bow as need drove him to his rich cousin.

It was seven in the morning. The factory was not yet open. Zalman wandered along Park Avenue; on one side were factories, garages, a veterinary hospital; on the other side, between iron fences, a line of railroad tracks. He stopped at the fence to watch. A train sped by, leaving behind it the echo of wheels on the rails. Not a blade of grass, not a tree. Dusty, colorless gravel, surrounded by faded walls, fire-escapes, greasy windows. Telegraph wires hummed, merging with the rattling of milk-and-bread wagons. And above the buildings, above the street, an occasional factory-chimney blew smoke rings.

Zalman raised his head, peered at the deep-blue sky and muttered gloomily: "It's May again."

The word itself affected him. He drew himself up, wanted

to get outside himself, wanted to get inside a life which was far away from him. His eyes searched among the paving stones. Here a new blade of grass, there a new blade of grass. The early-morning air was full of unrest, of spring, of aromas which get to the soul. The memory of a piece of life of a quarter-century ago came over him.

It was May. Zalman and David, ten years old, had gone off at dawn to the railroad station on the other side of the woods for a picnic. The dawn smelled of dew, of elderberries, of blossoming birch-trees. At the refreshment-booth they drank fresh milk, ate rye-bread with butter, believed the attendant when he told them that May mornings bring happiness, bring luck, drive away all man's sorrows.

The odors, human odors, of a quarter-century ago, drove Zalman now to David, to his own cousin. Hadn't they grown up together? Weren't they brothers of a sort? One does not let a brother down.

Less dejected now, Zalman entered the factory. Not asking questions of anyone, he made straight for the office. A worker stopped him.

"Whom do you wish to see?"

"Mister Fagin."

"He isn't here yet."

"Can you tell me when he's expected?"

"What do you want to see him about?"

"I'm his cousin."

"His cousin?" The office-worker measured him with a suspicious eye and said: "You can wait here. Mister Fagin should be in any minute."

The oppressive factory, the rows of workers standing over the half-finished mattresses, began to disperse Zalman's previous mood. He walked toward the exit, hoping to meet David on the street.

An automobile had stopped outside the factory. Fagin, a

stoutish man in a light suit, got out of the car. Zalman tried to find the piece of life that had awakened in him that morning; he wanted to offer it to David. But it had dissolved. His mood extinguished, Zalman took a step toward his cousin.

"Hello, Dave."

Dave turned his head to see who had spoken. He looked at his cousin and started to puff on the cigar stuck casually in a corner of his mouth. For a moment he hesitated, then, like a boss, said:

"How's life treating you, Zalman?"

"Not so good."

"Not working?"

"Nothing in the last eight months."

"Not so good is right."

Dave Fagin busied himself locking the car-door. It disturbed Zalman. He suspected that the last thing David wanted now was for his cousin to come up to his office. Why didn't he say something? He felt Dave's hand on his arm.

"Zalman, do you need a few dollars?"

Neither of them said a word. Their faces were alike, the faces of actual brothers. For an instant they looked into each other's eyes. Then Zalman, not asking, but demanding, said:

"I want a job in your factory, Dave!"

"A job?" Dave drew on his cigar, blew out quick puffs of smoke, and every wrinkle in his face seemed to be considering the question. "What are we standing out here for? Come on up!"

In the office, Dave took off his coat and hat and, not sitting down, looked through the mail his secretary had prepared for him. Then he said to her:

"Miss Rose, see that we're not disturbed for a while!"

When they were alone, and had seated themselves on either side of the desk, Dave put his cigar down on an ash-

tray. He picked up a pencil, twirled it in his fingers and said:
"Apparently you don't know how much a mattress-worker makes, Zalman. A good hand can earn eighteen-twenty dollars a week tops. The average is fourteen, sixteen . . . But you won't make even that. You're a beginner in the trade, a learner."

"So what?" Zalman minimized all the difficulties. "It'll take a week, or two, and I'll learn the whole profession. You say they don't make much? And if I've been without work for more than half-a-year, is that better?"

While Zalman spoke, Dave had written down a column of figures on an envelope. He suddenly crossed them out and leaned all the way across the desk.

"Listen, Zalman. You can have the job, but only if you agree to change your name."

"Why change my name?" Zalman asked as his eyes clouded.

"I don't like the idea of a cousin of mine working in a — "

"But if it's allright with me —"

"Maybe it's allright with you." Dave threw the pencil down on the desk. "But not with me. I, the owner of the factory, am Mr. Fagin, and you, my cousin, a mere apprentice, also Mr. Fagin. It doesn't make sense!"

"Nobody has to know we're cousins!" Zalman's blood began to pound in his temples.

"Certainly nobody in the factory has to know it." Dave's mouth relaxed. "So don't be a fool! Change your name."

"No!"

"Then you can't work here."

"You can go to hell!" Zalman leaped from his chair.

"If that's the way you feel about it, then we're quits! Goodbye!" Dave paled as he pointed toward the door.

"Listen, Mr. Fagin," said Zalman, fury in his eyes, in his hands, as he bent over the desk toward his cousin, who merely placed his finger on a button at the edge of his desk.

"Listen, Mr. Fagin, you can go to hell with all your money and your whole damn factory!"

Two men came running into the office and hustled Zalman out to the street.

How the Fight Began

by JOSEPH OPATOSHU

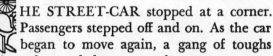

THE STREET-CAR stopped at a corner. Passengers stepped off and on. As the car began to move again, a gang of toughs pushed in noisily and sprawled out over the seats.

They talked loudly, shoved each other, all the while baiting and harassing one of their number, the skinniest and smallest in the gang. The victim's eyes leaped foolishly as he tried to see who was whacking his head from behind. He tried to get away, but they kept shoving and poking him mockingly from all sides. The other people in the car were amused by these antics. But the young victim finally hung his head like a whipped dog.

Suddenly he looked up and pointed to a peddler sitting in the car. "Sheeny! Look at the sheeny-beard!"

Across from him sat an old Jew, a peddler, with baskets

hung across his shoulders. He seemed to be trying to make himself smaller and smaller so that he would take up less space. His eyes darted here and there like those of a scared rabbit as he tried to avoid the glances of those around him. Whenever the car shook, the baskets on his shoulders banged against his teeth.

The gang of toughs immediately forgot about their previous victim and studied the peddler for a few moments. Then, having looked at each other knowingly, they began to laugh in a way that curdled the old man's blood.

The skinny boy, in an obvious effort to regain his lost esteem, leaped across the car and grabbed the Jew's beard. Growling like a dog before he barks, he snarled through his teeth:

"Whis-kers! Whis-kers!"

The Jew whacked him across the hand and the gang almost danced for joy.

"Kiss the sheeny! Kiss the sheeny!"

Inside the car, everything had grown deadly quiet. The few Jews in the car hid their faces behind their newspapers, trying to go unnoticed.

But one pale young man got up and faced the skinny tough, his eyes blazing as though they were about to pop out of his head.

"What did that old man ever do to you?"

The tough let go the peddler's beard, seemingly taken aback by the young man's eyes, and started to turn away. One of the gang called out:

"What's it his business, Bill? He must be a sheeny, too!"

"Give him one on the nose!"

"Rap him in the eye, Bill!"

"What're you waitin' for, Bill?"

"Attaway, Bill! Now you're doin' it!"

The young man felt a blow on his cheek that knocked him

back to one of the seats. He tried to get up again, but found himself wrestling with one of the gang who was pinning him down.

The skinny one meanwhile had resumed his harassment of the old peddler, pulling his beard and calling him names. The old man tried to push him away as he berated him in Yiddish.

"Gangster! What did I ever do to you?"

The passengers in the car looked on coldly. Some of them smiled a little as though they were watching two boys in a street fight. The few Jews in the car buried their heads deeper in their newspapers, looking up nervously at the scene, trembling in fear and angry agitation. But fear was strong enough to keep them frozen in their places.

Suddenly a young woman appeared in the midst of the toughs and began to tug at the one who was tormenting the peddler.

"You ought to be ashamed of yourself, you bully! What did this old man do to you? You're only tough because he can't defend himself! You call yourself an American?"

The peddler looked up at her gratefully.

One of the gang came to the young woman's help and also pulled at the skinny one. "OK, Bill, let him alone! Can't you see the lady wants you to let the sheeny alone!"

"Yeah, I'll let him alone! But first he has to promise to shave off his sheeny whiskers!" He turned to the old man. "I'll even give you a quarter for the barber!"

"I'm a sheeny, too!" the young woman exclaimed. "And if any one of you comes near me I'll slap his face!"

"Aha! A sheeny lady!" The whole gang immediately surrounded her. "Slap me first!" said the skinny one, as he reached for the peddler's beard.

She slapped him so hard that the sound reverberated through the car.

"Three cheers for the lady!" one of the passengers called out.

A tough brandished his fist at her.

"Keep your dirty hands off her!" came a cry from another part of the car. The Jews behind their newspapers threw them away and clenched their fists.

And that's how the fight began . . .

ISAAC RABOI

ISAAC RABOI

1883-1944

Raboi came to the United States in 1904, along with thousands of other Jewish immigrants, but his experiences in the new country were different from those of his writer-colleagues. After a couple of years as a frame-maker for ladies hats, and as a fur worker, he grew sick of city life and decided to study farming. He enrolled at the Baron de Hirsch Agricultural School at Woodbine, New Jersey, and after he finished his course there, took a job on a ranch in North Dakota. Then, for a while, he managed a family farm which his father bought in Connecticut. But in 1913 this farm failed and the family was forced to move back to New York. Isaac returned to the ladies' hat trade for his livelihood.

During this time he had begun to write for various Yiddish periodicals and was considered one of *"Di Yunge"*—The Youth —a group of new writers who had publicly dissociated themselves from the old schools of Yiddish writing. "At that time, the *Yunge* were a bright phenomenon on the American-Jewish horizon. A sharp change in Jewish life had to have occurred—like the emigration and the proletarianization of the Jewish masses—in order for such a group of writers to arise 'suddenly' . . . And from them came a crop of poets and storytellers of a breadth never before seen in Yiddish literature. How happy I was to be one of the *Yunge!* . . . Whoever was publishing any kind of literary journal asked me to contribute something . . ." (*My Life*, 2 vols. New York, 1945-7)

Raboi's approach to the new life in America was different from that of the other Yiddish writers. "When Raboi's hero came to America, he made no tragedy out of it. His *'Nine Brothers'* were sturdy Bessarabian youths who had hardly missed the traditions and customs they had left behind . . They looked forward, not backward . . . Raboi's hero did not remain stuck on the East Side—he became a Jewish Cowboy in the West, a farmer in New England . . . He added new American fruits to Yiddish writing . . ." (I. E. Ronch, *America in Yiddish Literature*, New York 1945)

Isaac Leads A Strike

by ISAAC RABOI

*(A chapter from "Nine Brothers".
Isaac's trade, the frame-makers for
ladies hats, has called a strike)*

URING THE FIRST DAYS of the general strike Isaac felt like a soldier in training. He got up in the morning while the blue dawn still showed outside his window. When Mama heard Isaac tiptoeing through the house she, too, got up to make him his coffee and soft-boiled eggs. Isaac was never hungry so early in the day. But Mama hovered over him until he had to finish his breakfast if only to please her. Mama also managed to slip a few coins into his coat pocket.

"Again you'll be out all day and all night! How long will this go on?"

"Until we win," Isaac told her simply.

The day began with "guard duty" outside the shop, to prevent the bosses from bringing in scabs. All the workers in the shop were expected to fulfill this obligation. In the few days since the strike had begun, Isaac had gotten to recognize everyone who habitually went in and out of the building. Whenever a new face appeared, Isaac followed up the steps until he saw exactly where the person was heading. There were two other shops in the building, a handbag shop and a wallet-and-purse factory. Isaac had studied the faces of the men and women in those two shops until he considered himself an expert on the subject. When the workers began to arrive in the morning, the strikers took up their positions to watch. But without Isaac they were lost.

"Who's *she?*"

"She's allright. She works in handbags."

Wachenblau's had shut down tight. Sam the Foreman seemed to have disappeared. He had not been seen in the shop for several days. Instead, Mr. Wachenblau himself made an appearance. He floated through the lines of strikers in a kind of disembodied manner, with his long cigar between his lips and a flat straw hat on his head. Whenever Isaac tried to picture him later, all he could see was a hat and a cigar. The bookkeeper also smuggled herself into the building every morning. Once Isaac blocked her way at the entrance.

"Listen, girl. What's doing up there?"

"Nothing!" Her eyes darted here and there apprehensively to see whether anyone had seen her talking to a striker.

"You're sure nobody's working up there?"

"Positive. Nobody at all."

"And where's Sam?"

"I don't know!"

"What kind of answer is that! You may be a bookkeeper, but if we want to pull you out we can do that, too! The only reason we let you stay up there is to get information for us!"

"Please, let me go now. I'm telling you the truth. It's getting late. Sam is staying at home, in his own house. Maybe he had an argument with Mister Wachenblau . . ."

"So you do know something! Don't be scared, we won't give you away. Try to find out what they argued about and let me know as soon as you can. Now go on up and keep your eyes open!"

As she went inside, the other strikers gathered around Isaac.

"What did she have to say?"

"They've already started fighting amongst themselves!"

"Who?"

"Sam and the boss!"

"Good! I hope they tear each other apart!"

"Maybe he'll fire him!"

"No more foreman!"

"So what? Another louse will take his place!"

To Isaac, the bookkeeper's story smelled fishy. What would Sam be doing at home? But he did not want to communicate his doubts to the others. No use making them lose hope. The morale of the strike was still sound and militant. But Isaac was certain Sam was up to something. He decided to discuss it with Yaffe, the other strike leader. The strikers had already nicknamed them: The Towhead and the Gypsy. Isaac was sunburned and blackhaired. Yaffe, pale and blond. But the two friends paid little attention to the jokes.

"You know something, Yaffe, I'm afraid Sam has moved the shop to his house." Isaac spoke in a whisper.

"What makes you think so?"

"I could read it in the bookkeeper's face."

"It makes sense. But how could you read that in somebody's face—" Yaffe laughed.

"She let it slip that Sam was home. I could see she was sorry she said it even before the words were out of her mouth."

"Well, we'll have to make sure."

"But keep it quiet!" cautioned Isaac.

"We'll have to do it ourselves."

"But we don't know where he lives."

"She'll have to tell us. Why didn't you ask her?"

"I didn't think of it! But it's not such a good idea anyway. Suppose she goes to the boss with the story?"

"You're right. We'll have to find out from one of the men—"

"But we can't let them know why we want the address!"

Yaffe volunteered to do the "undercover work." They agreed that it had to be done with extreme caution.

It was almost time to relieve the pickets. For the rest of the morning it was not necessary to keep everybody in front of the shop. Most of them would now walk over to the beer-saloon which housed their "headquarters." That would be the time for Yaffe to drop a word about Sam. He would say that he had seen the foreman on Seventh Avenue. Then Isaac would ask whether Sam lived on that street. Yaffe would say he thought so. If he chose the right moment when all the men were listening, most likely one of them would come up with Sam's correct address.

"But suppose none of them knows it?" Yaffe asked.

"Then we'll have to think of another way!"

But it worked out according to plan. Among the strikers was an old hand who remembered Wachenblau when he still had a little shop on Bond Street. Sam had been an ordinary frame-maker then. As Yaffe and Isaac had hoped, the old man supplied the information.

"I shouldn't know where he feeds his ugly face?" he chortled. There was a big gap in his mouth where his bottom teeth should have been.

So Isaac and Yaffe were put on the right track. After one o'clock they took a walk on Sam's street until they found the house. Then they stationed themselves nearby and waited to see who would go in and come out. For two hours they saw only mothers taking care of their children—nursing them, chasing them, scolding them, rocking them in baby carriages. But Isaac and Yaffe wanted to be certain. A few doors from the house was a butcher shop. They waited until the store was empty of customers and then went in to talk with the butcher.

"Hello!"

"Hello!" The butcher inspected them with two tiny blue eyes and wiped his hands on his blood-smeared apron.

"Could you tell us whether Sam lives on this street?"

"Sam? There's only one Sam on this street? Or only one red cow in the world? There's three or four Sams here. Which one do you want?"

As they described their foreman, the butcher grew visibly alarmed. He picked up his big butcher-knife.

"Mister! You don't have to be afraid of us—we're only strikers!"

"Oh!" he breathed. His face relaxed in relief. "Strikers? Why didn't you say so right away? In that case, talk with all your teeth! I thought you were from his—you know—" He laid the knife back on the scarred butcher-block and wiped his hands again on his greasy pants. Then he shook hands with them.

"For strikers I'll do anything I can!"

"Good. Do you know whether anything unusual is going on in Sam's house? We think maybe he set up a shop there—"

"It shouldn't be hard to find out. I'll go up and take a look. I'm an innocent man. What do I know about his business? I'll just go up to ask his mother if she wants a fresh cut of chuck. I've done it before. Leave it to me, boys. Wait here!"

The butcher left the store in their care. Isaac and Yaffe, for the first time that day, looked at each other doubtfully and considered what they had gotten themselves into.

"What'll we do if he tells Sam we're down here?" asked

Yaffe. He was always the more practical of the two. But it was too late anyway. Even if they took to their heels now they would be caught.

Isaac's philosophy was to accept people as honest until they proved otherwise. But as Yaffe said, it was too late for discussions. The butcher was already coming back. He was alone, and they took that for a good sign.

"Somebody sold you a bill of goods!" he laughed as he came back into the store. "There's nobody working up there. The phonograph's playing to split your eardrums and Sam's stretched out on the sofa with his mouth open!"

When he had finished his report, the two simpletons (as the butcher had crowned them in his own mind) exchanged glances, said goodbye to their ally and left.

They arrived at the saloon just as the men were preparing to return to the shops for the mass picketing. As they came out into the street, a striker came running up to them.

"Scabs!" he cried breathlessly. "Scabs in our shop!"

"Goldstein Brothers?"

"Yes! Scabs!"

The executive committee considered the new situation. Tony's face paled. "Break their goddam necks!"

"No," said Koylin. "Not that way." He was opposed to violence on principle.

"How else? You want me to pat their little heads?"

"Maybe we can talk to them first. Maybe they don't even know there's a strike."

"Break their goddam necks!" insisted Tony.

It was late afternoon. All day the sun had baked the asphalt. The street was hot and glowing, like an oven. The strikers marched two and three abreast, noisily. Passers-by paused, curious to learn what was going on.

At the factory which housed "Goldstein Brothers" they stopped and formed a big semi-circle outside the narrow six-story building. The front of the building was covered with black marble. The windows, high and rounded at the top, were all open. The noise of the machines came pouring out into the street. It seemed to Isaac as though the machines on each floor had purposefully agreed not to work in the same rhythm. When the machines on the top-floor momentarily stopped their scraping of a thousand saws, a whining whirr began on another floor, as though a giant drill were boring into the heart of the earth. The ground around the building shook. The entire granite structure trembled, especially the first-floor windows with the gold inscription: GOLDSTEIN BROTHERS.

No sooner had the crowd of pickets with their bare heads and rolled-up shirt-sleeves taken their places outside the shop, when a face flashed in one of the open windows and something came hurtling toward the sidewalk. A plaster-block hit the cement with a crash and shattered into a million pieces. On the way down it grazed the shoulder of a picket.

What happened next nobody had foreseen. A roar came from the pickets and they made for the door of the building as though they were shot from a cannon. The door was locked. The enraged pickets refused to be stopped by a locked door; it gave way and fell into the shop along with the man.

The shop was long and narrow, like the building itself. The light from the windows carried only half way across the room; the other half was in shadow. The brothers Goldstein and the "scabs," plaster blocks in hand, had barricaded themselves in the dark half of the room.

Tony led the strikers' attack. He leaped across the room at one of the scabs, grabbed the block from his hand and smashed it down on his head. The hollow block, shaped like a lady's hat, split into bits and scattered over the floor.

The battle began in earnest. Screams and curses. Swinging fists. Plaster blocks flew like bullets back and forth between the two warring camps.

"Police are coming!" somebody yelled.

The strikers leaped toward the doorway and hurdled the fallen door like stags taking a fence. When the police arrived, not one of the strikers was left in the shop. They found only the brothers Goldstein with their heads cracked and the scabs with bruised fingers and bloody noses. The shop was a wreck. Ambulance-bells clanged on the street. White-coated doctors wound bandages. Crowds came running, hoping to see the casualties carried out on stretchers.

Later that evening the strikers held a general meeting in the saloon. They sat on chairs, tables, window-sills. All the doors were open wide. The heat in the place was suffocating. Each shop had assigned one speaker to report. The strike leadership sat at a table nearest the front door. The air pulsated with life and courage. It was enough for a speaker to crack a feeble joke and the result was a gale of laughter and applause.

A policeman suddenly appeared at the open door, behind him an assortment of strange-looking creatures with swollen heads wrapped in muslin. Blackened eyes and bloody tips of noses stuck out of the bandages. The strikers took one look at this vision and roared.

Even the policeman was embarrassed. The big white heads moved among the strikers, the sunken eyes searching feverishly from out of the white muslin. But they could not identify anyone. The strikers had carried out their unplanned attack-and-retreat with such swiftness that the victims did not know who had hit them.

They made another unsuccessful tour of the crowd and then slunk out of the saloon, the cop following sheepishly behind.

Mister Goldenbarg Settles In the West

by Isaac Raboi

(Chapter from "Mister Goldenbarg," a novella)

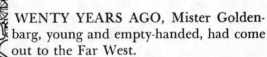

TWENTY YEARS AGO, Mister Goldenbarg, young and empty-handed, had come out to the Far West.

His young wife, Rachel, had stayed behind in the big city. She had told him to "take his time." When he would write her that he had found something good, she would come out to join him.

In the Dakotas, he selected a homestead of 160 acres of land on which no human being had set foot since primeval times. He selected this particular piece of land for many reasons. First, it extended over a flat plain, with a high, broad hill at its northern end. Second, right through the middle of it flowed a good-sized stream. And third, the soil was rich, and the grass grew high.

There were other reasons, innumerable reasons, and he

fell in love with it.

All alone he walked across the broad stretches of land, thinking things out and making his plans. At first he decided to build his house close by the stream, but then he thought better of it. He would build the house at the foot of the hill. He could get water elsewhere. But at the foot of the hill it would be warmer in the wintertime, protected from the winds.

And on the day they handed him the papers in the government office and told him about the conditions: that first, he must build a house, and second, dig a well, and third, plow up five acres of land and seed them, and fourth and most important, that he must settle on the land and make his home there—when they raised all these things with him—Mister Goldenbarg nodded agreement to each point and said nothing and signed the papers.

What he wanted to say, from the depths of his heart, he could not express. So he signed the papers dumbly.

Then he wrote his Rachel a short but happy note: "Dearest Rachel, I have found a good piece of land. Get ready to leave. I'm starting to build. . . ."

And as soon as he mailed the letter to his wife he already felt at home on the naked prairie. He called on his closest neighbor, Mister Elkins, who had two horses and a good farm, and introduced himself.

"What can I do for you?" his neighbor asked him amiably.

"First I'd like to do something for *you,* then you can repay the favor," replied Mister Goldenbarg.

Elkins was offended. "That's not the way we do things out here. We don't keep accounts. Whatever you need done I'll do for you gladly. And when *I* need something done, I believe you will do it just as gladly for me. . . ."

"I will, I will . . .," Goldenbarg murmured. He did not understand the difference.

First off, Elkins rode into town with him and they brought back a wagonload of boards, shingles, and other necessary materials. And Goldenbarg had to sleep and eat at the Elkins'; they would not hear of anything else. And in honor of the new neighbor, Mrs. Elkins killed a hen and roasted some beef and potatoes.

"You *are* a Jew and you don't eat pork," she said significantly.

On the third day, Mr. Elkins rode out with horse and plow and turned up a stretch of Goldenbarg's land. Every day for a week he did this, until he had plowed up five acres.

In the meantime, Mister Goldenbarg took his new axe and went down into a deep valley and cut down some willow trees. He carried them back on his shoulders and piled them in a stack near the spot where he was going to build his house. When he had accumulated a pile of logs, he chopped them into kindling.

Then one day Elkins drove him into town again and they brought back a wagonload of seed potatoes. It was still not too late in the season to plant potatoes.

Soon his name was going from mouth to mouth among all his neighbors. When a neighbor would ride by and see the growing pile of logs bleaching in the sun, and the acres of plowed land increasing, he would tell about this in town.

And when they planted the potatoes, Goldenbarg did it with undisguised fervor, carefully placing each slice of tuber with the peel up. This, and the manner in which he did the work, pleased Mister Elkins exceedingly, and he talked about it to his neighbors in the town.

Later, a week before the potato leaves began to sprout, Elkins helped him set up the framework of his house. Whereupon Goldenbarg took Elkins' hand and tried to kiss it. He did not know how to thank this Gentile enough for all the help he had given him.

His work proceeded according to a schedule. At sunrise he would start work on the house. He built it all by himself. At sundown he would put down his building tools and go to work on the potatoes, weeding and cultivating by the light of the moon.

So they talked about this in the town and the Jew Goldenbarg soon acquired a good name and they began to foresee much wealth and a good home.

Later, when he finished building the house, which consisted of a large square room and a small kitchen with a brick oven, and when he had dug the well and lined it with stones, and all the neighbors came and admired his work, Mister Goldenbarg sent for his wife.

The first day that Mister Goldenbarg's wife came west, he conducted her over the plains and hills and valleys of their new home.

At the edge of the potato field they stood for a long time, gazing wordlessly. Rachel could not tear her eyes away from the neatness of the rows and the high, thick, verdant stems of the dark-green potato plants.

When she grew thirsty after all the walking, he took her over to the well and pulled up a pail of water for her. She drank the cool water and rested and drank again and her heart was delighted.

And when they then climbed to the top of the hill and looked out over everything that was "theirs" and at what Mister Goldenbarg had done with his own bare hands in such a short time, Rachel felt as though she had been kidnapped from a poor hovel by a Prince and brought to live in a luxurious palace.

That same evening all their neighbors from the nearby countryside came to visit. She sensed that there were no Jews among them, that she was the only Jewish woman here. . . . Anxiety tapped lightly at her heart.

She was still very young then. Goldenbarg had met her in New York and married her "with one dress to her name." But she was pretty and she had come to America as a little girl. And yet, even though she was something of a "Yankee" herself, she felt a bit ill-at-ease among this assortment of new neighbors.

The neighbors, however, did not even notice it. In a very short time—as women will do—they told her all about the ways and customs of the Far West.

Rachel listened to everything, smiling shyly at this one and gazing admiringly at that one.

The countryside there is vast and expansive, but when one rides into town he is never too busy to stop at a neighbor's house and knock at the door and talk with the woman of the house and tell her what happened here and what happened there. In this way, news travels from house to house, and very quickly.

The news of Mrs. Goldenbarg's arrival sped across the prairie to all their neighbors and it only served to strengthen their confidence in Goldenbarg's complete success.

Mister Goldenbarg soon bought two horses and a long, green wagon and a harvesting machine and many other things—all of which he was asked to accept on credit. And since he had faith in his ability to pay, he bought whatever he needed.

The first crop he harvested was his hay. The grass was as high as his head. For thousands of years the land had lain here and yielded its fruits, year in and year out, of its own accord. The long winters covered it with deep snows, the earth grew richer and richer, and each year the grasses grew higher and higher.

So Mister Goldenbarg reaped the hay and his wife followed behind him with a wooden pitchfork. And from time to time, whenever the tall grass jammed the machine, she cleaned it out with her fork.

And when the time came to stack the hay, Mrs. Goldenbarg tied a red kerchief around her neck, put a broad-brimmed hat on her head and went out into the fields to help her husband. She stood up in the wagon and he handed her the hay from the piles.

She noticed something. Every time he speared a forkful of hay, it seemed to her that he could manage even better if he would do as a woman does when she combs her long hair: he ought first to gather up all the stray ends of the hay and bring them together into the center, and then he would be able to lift the entire pile without losing a blade.

Goldenbarg was delighted with this idea, and, grinning at the womanly notion, he would gather the loose ends together with his pitchfork and then lift the pile high over the rim of the wagon, and with each lift a funny little sound would come out of his lips.

When they stacked the hay they would change jobs. She would stand in the wagon and hand the pitchforks of hay down to her husband. Goldenbarg would snatch it out of the fork and skillfully bale it and stack each bale in place.

Now it was his turn to notice something. The person handing down the hay must remember to point the fork teeth downward, so that the hay would come off without hindrance.

Mrs. Goldenbarg had a Yiddish proverb for this. *Voss tsu menner un voss tsu veiber* . . ."Men's affairs to men and women's to women."

Goldenbarg set up the bales in such a way that they would serve as a shield against the winds coming from the north. He covered them with a narrow, sharply-sloping roof so that the rain would run off quickly and not rot the hay. God's blessing lay stored in that hay, as well as in the potato field.

From each row of potatoes they dug out ten sacks.

A buyer came calling on Mister Goldenbarg, and when he heard there were a thousand sacks of potatoes, he offered him a dollar a sack on the spot.

Goldenbarg sold the potatoes and put the money into the bank in town.

The whole town rocked.

First off, he paid all his debts. Then he started building a stable for his horses. And he bought a cow, so that there might be milk in the house.

That's the way it went, year in, year out.

And when Goldenbarg looked around and saw that there was still enough free land on all sides, he selected a piece which adjoined his, and Mrs. Goldenbarg signed the government papers saying that she wanted it for a home for herself. Everybody else in the vicinity had done the same thing, so why not he?

The government gave her the piece of land, in accordance with the law, and their farm was doubled.

Some time later a government man came from the State and called a meeting of all homesteaders and made the following announcement:

"Whoever will plant one acre of trees on his land—fruit trees or any other kind of trees—will receive free from the government just as much land again as he now owns."

What farmer could pass up an opportunity like that?

Mister Goldenbarg planted several rows of maple trees in the northwest corner of his property and his land doubled again. Whereupon, his crop increased and he found he could not do all the work himself; he needed a helper.

So every year he would bring in from the big city of New York a strong young fellow, Jewish, because "a Jew doesn't get drunk and become undependable." But the Jewish fellows never stayed long; one year, and then they grew homesick for the big city, and off they went.

Until God sent him Isaac, a young man who worked with honest diligence, like one of the family. . . .

BORUCH GLASMAN

BORUCH GLASMAN

1893-1945

Boruch Glasman came to the United States in 1911 full of learning and visions. Anxious to continue his studies, he supported himself by teaching in Hebrew Schools while he attended college. He wrote a few stories in English which were published in various Jewish periodicals, but nothing further came of this. His first love was Yiddish. He longed for a Yiddish-speaking environment and he wanted nothing better than to write for Yiddish-speaking Jews.

For this reason he left the United States for a time to live in Poland, where his fellow Jews spoke the language which was "music to his ears." After a few years, convinced that the culture of Europe's Yiddish-speaking Jewry would eventually have its effect on New York, he returned to the United States. Here he consciously tried to make his work reflect America—not only New York, but the greater American landscape, including Jews who had been here for generations.

He was one of the first Yiddish writers to deal with the theme of the Negro in this country.

Like other Yiddish writers of his generation, Glasman was tormented by the problems facing Jews in the United States —the future of Yiddish, the decay of tradition, the undue influence of wealth upon the values of the community. Glasman himself described the problems this way: "One would like to concretize, to fix, our variegated life here, although it is difficult to do that with something that is in the process of . . . being reforged. We face changes here that can be compared only to the period when we stood at the threshold of the Spanish period of our history . . . And whatever else you may say, we are certainly not creating any new ghettos here in the European style!"

The story in this selection, *"Goat in the Backyard,"* is not typical of Glasman, nor is its deliberate, almost childlike style. Perhaps for that very reason it succeeds in evoking an immediate sympathetic involvement, not only with the little girl, but with the goat as well.

Goat in the Backyard

by BORUCH GLASMAN

IN NEW YORK CITY live many newcomers, people who were not born here in America, but in countries across the ocean. Among them are also many Jews and Italians.

On a small, remote street in the Bronx lived two such families, one Italian and one Jewish. The street was far from the busy part of town, with many little gardens and trees. The surrounding streets were not yet built up. They had been cut through rock and stone, and along the sides of the streets you could still see sections of untouched rock which had lain here undisturbed for millions of years, one layer atop another, like a birthday cake.

The city of New York is built on rock, and the people who live there have gradually become hardened, too.

Evenings, the Italian man used to rest on the porch of his

little house. He was a street-cleaner. All day long he cleaned the streets, other people's streets. On the job, he was dressed in a white suit and looked different from other people. But in the evening he would come home, wash up, change into ordinary clothing and begin to look like a human being, just like all other human beings.

He had a little garden where he planted cabbage and corn, lettuce and beets, onions and radishes, carrots and beans— all sorts of beans of the most varied colors, smooth and spotted, on bushes and on stakes. It gave him a great deal of pleasure to putter about his garden, because it was *his* garden, a garden he had planted with his own hands.

But on this particular evening he sat on his porch, sad and pensive. Autumn had already arrived. Everything in the garden had been taken down. Here and there, sticks of various heights jutted out of the upturned soil. Only the cabbage-heads now stuck out of the ground, red and purple, blue and orange. The colors of the cabbage in these autumn days changed from hour to hour, almost as quickly as the colors in the sky during a sunset. It was remarkable to look upon.

There was nothing for the Italian man now to do in his garden. So he sat on his porch in the evenings, feeling sad. And because he felt so sad, he was homesick. He longed for Italy, for the country from which he came. In Italy he had lived in wild, hilly country. In his mind he could see the light-drenched columns amidst the ruins of ancient palaces and buildings still standing in his town. He had owned a fruit-orchard and a good-sized garden. The garden hung at the edge of a cliff over a brown sea. The hills were wild and he had hunted wild goats. When he caught one he would domesticate it. It takes a lot of strength and patience to tame a wild goat.

So on this particular evening the thought occurred to him

—why not keep a goat here in America, too? He couldn't go out and catch a wild one, but he could still *buy* a goat. From the goat's milk he could churn his own cheese; Italians do so love cheese made out of goat-milk.

Thus, one night when the weather had grown cooler and the first snow had fallen, through the bare gardens and rocky streets of the neighborhood echoed the meh-meh of a goat.

* * *

On the same street lived a Jewish family—father, mother and their little daughter. The daughter's name was Mary. But her mother used to call here Mereleh. Sometimes, Mother would joke: Mereleh—Mereleh—today we have a *mereleh-tsimmis* for supper. In Yiddish, you see, a "mereleh" is a little carrot.

Mereleh had once had a little sister, but she had died. Ever since, it often happened that Mereleh could not sleep. During the night she would wake up suddenly and not be able to fall asleep again. She would wonder where her little sister could be now. She knew that her sister had died, but where had she gone? Where could she be now at night while she, Mereleh, lay in her snug little bed asleep or awake?

And as Mereleh lay thinking these thoughts, she heard the meh-meh of a goat. It may be that she was the very first person in the street to hear the bleating of that goat. Barefoot, in her nightgown, she went to look out the window.

Outdoors, it was blue overhead and white underfoot. And somewhere nearby, in the dark stillness of the street, a goat was crying.

In the Italian man's yard stood a little shed with a sloping roof. A hole was cut into a side of the shed. Mereleh could see the goat stepping in and out. The goat was grey, with black spots, and her horns curled back to her neck. She was tied by a rope to the shed. The goat did not know what to make of this fact and cried out in the night—meh-meh—what is this on my horns which keeps me from running where I like . . .

She paced at the end of the rope like a night-spirit, leaving signs of her feet in the snow and cries of meh-meh in the air. She thought and thought, and shook her little beard in the light of the moon . . .

That night Mereleh could not fall asleep at all. Wherever had the goat come from? It was tied with a rope. Why had they tied it with a rope? Probably so that it wouldn't run away. But why should the goat want to run away? Probably because she was afraid somebody might hurt her. But why would anyone want to hurt a goat? The Italian must be a cruel man, so he tied up the goat with a rope to keep her from running away. Where could she run away to, even if they untied the rope? Where does a goat come from?

The neighbors who rose early that morning and heard the bleating of the goat didn't know where the goat came from either. But that didn't prevent them from being delighted with it. In the middle of their housework the women heard the goat's meh-meh and went running to their back windows. Goats are a rare sight in a big city; city-people always enjoy looking at goats or cows or sheep. City-people cast their mind's eye back to distant places and see themselves in a field, or a woods. Many of the people in this very street had themselves once lived near fields or woods.

Mereleh's father had not been born in America. He was born in Lithuania, in a small town in the middle of wide, flat, barren fields. All around the town stretched nothing but fields and fields. A hill was a rarity. A tree, a solitary tree standing by itself out in the middle of a field, gave you such a lonely feeling you wanted to cry.

The streets of the town were narrow, sandy. If you ventured outside the town the fields would suddenly stretch out before you all the way to the edge of the sky as far as you could see. The ground was so low and flat it made you sad to look at it. Your heart would start to ache and you would want to get away from there and walk and walk without stopping across the flat fields, day and night, day and night . . .

Mereleh's father had grown up a quiet man, a good man, a sad man. He never said much. But not out of anger. Out of goodness. He did not like to raise his voice—as though he were a little frightened. When he had been a child at home, in Lithuania, he would spend all day in the *cheder*. And in the winter time, all his evenings, too. The *cheder* was dirty and crowded. All day the *rebbe* would scold and scream. At home, life was poor.

Mereleh's father, when he was a boy, spent very little time playing. Always he would be sitting and reading. He ran away from goats, more often than not. A goat was wild. That was an expression—"wild as a goat." A goat could scoop up a child on its horns and carry it off. Goats used to roam around the town cemetery, cropping the grass around the graves. Some of the boys would jump up on the goats and ride them. The goats would try to escape. They would cry and beg the boys to let them go. Mereleh's father used to plead with his friends to stop tormenting the poor goats. But they paid no attention to him. They laughed at him. Then he would run away and cry his heart out. He stopped playing with his friends and grew even quieter than before.

Mereleh was a lot like her father.

* * *

But it didn't take long and the goat in Mereleh's street stopped its meh-meh-ing. Mereleh begged her mother to go across to the Italian man and buy some of the cheese he had made out of the goat's milk. Mereleh was an only child and her mother loved her very much. So she went over to the Italian man to buy the cheese.

But she came right back, looking at Mereleh with a big grin. The Italian did not have any cheese yet, Mama reported, because the goat had not given any milk yet. Wait, Mereleh. Soon Spring will be here and the nannygoat will have a baby goat, maybe two baby goats. The goat will be a mama, just as I am *your* mama. Then she will give milk and the Italian man will make cheese . . .

And soon the Spring did come. Suddenly, all at once, unexpectedly, as Spring always comes to New York. Unexpectedly Spring comes. Dreamy-eyed she tries her first steps. But the attempt rarely succeeds. Winter returns. Spring tries a second time, a third time. The empty streets and the gardens behind the streets gradually take off their white clothes and put on green. The branches on the trees, and the twigs, cover themselves with leaves. Gradually the spaces between the branches are woven over with leaves and then the space between one tree and its neighbor is also woven over with leaves.

During the night a rain came and tapped on the roof. Slowly, persistently, merrily, bringing happy news. All night the rain fell, as though all the windows of heaven had opened at once. And Mereleh stood beneath the skylight in her house and listened to the tapping of the rain. From somewhere up high it came. The drops fell a long way and a long time, down, down, before they splashed happily on the roof.

As Mereleh stood listening, the rain stopped abruptly. And as it did she heard a faint, faint meh—as though the goat had taken sick and had no more strength to cry. Quiet. Then a tiny, tiny meh-eh, trembling, quivering, submissive, exactly like the sound of thin glass breaking. Mereleh's heart beat faster as she stood and listened . . .

Two days later, two baby goats were already dancing around the mama-goat. Both white, as though bathed in milk.

No horns yet, their legs long and thin, and their ears turned back. At first they were extremely cautious. They would suddenly take a little jump, as though someone had touched them with a match, and then would stand stock still, their small, shiny eyes bulging. They were positively amazed by the world, constantly discovering something new. Helter-skelter, with a hop, skip and jump, they would leap at each other, bang their heads together and then stop dead. Sometimes it would be a fence they banged, a tree, a log, a stone. But never a human being. From human beings they fled. That they were supposed to run away from humans they knew as soon as they were born, or even before.

All day long they played with each other. One would run, the other would chase. In a few days, they learned how to race pell-mell, leaping high in the air in an arc. The mama-goat would never have been able to catch them even if she had run after them. A human being certainly not. Close by the street rose a stony wall of rock, straight up, a bare wall rising up in a straight line. The little white goats would climb up the sharp bare stones. It was wonderful and frightening to watch. You would think—now, now—they will fall down. They would skip across the rocks, totter, then skip again. But they saw nothing, knew nothing. They would leap across the crevices and cut their feet on the sharp stones. Red blood would stain their whiteness but they would keep right on jumping.

The Italian man's little boy wanted to bandage the baby goats' bruised feet. But he couldn't catch them. He fell off the slippery rock and hurt himself. When he picked himself up he was terribly angry. And when he finally caught one of the goats he hit her so hard that he broke one of her legs. Then he carefully tied up the leg with a white bandage. In a few days the little goat again was skipping about, bandaged leg and all. She didn't mind a bit . . .

It was such a joy to watch the little goats. So young, so frisky. From early morning to late in the afternoon, as long as there was light, they would skip about all over the street, and when a neighbor sometimes grew downhearted, or when a child started crying, or sulking, they would only have to look through the window at the little goats. The grownups would start smiling and the children would laugh and applaud and join hands and dance in a circle, laughing and leaping about like the goats . . .

* * *

The little goats grew up. They would butt each other with their new horns, or simply leap in the air, or stand up on their hind legs, then let themselves down again, lower their heads and butt away. The mama-goat had already begun to teach them the correct way to do this. Goats must know this well, in case they should ever be attacked by a wild beast.

Mereleh used to stand at the window and watch. Whenever the goats would wander too far away and hide in the grass, the mama-goat would let out a low, uneasy cry: meh-eh-eh. She could not go chasing after them because she was tied up by a rope to a pole. But the little goats were free, because the Italian man knew they wouldn't really run away. Soon the goats would answer their mama, their high shaky voices as delicate and as trembling as that of little children showing off. They would appear amid the grass and leap at each other playfully over and over again.

Mereleh used to wonder. Each of the goats had a little sister to play with. She, too, would like to have a little sister to play with. But nevertheless she was happy for the little goats.

When her own Mama once asked her: Shall I go across to the Italian man and buy some goat cheese, she answered:

No, Mama, we don't need it. Let the baby goats have the milk. Little goats need milk, like little children.

Every day, Mereleh noticed how much bigger they were growing. Mereleh wanted very much for them to grow up. The Italian boy was always chasing after them, and when he caught one he would pester it unmercifully. But when they grew up, he would not be able to beat them, because their horns would grow bigger, too, and that's what goats' horns are for—for bad boys who won't let them alone.

The Italian had already made a lot of cheese out of the goat-milk. He put it out in the sun to dry, on a board laid across two high posts.

Summer was coming to a close. The Italian man sat on his porch one evening watching his goats play in the yard. I have enough cheese now for the whole winter, he thought. Next year the goat will have another little goat or two and I will have enough milk for more cheese.

He sat this way and watched and thought about his cheese. The little goats had grown up; they had filled out; their thin bones were covered with more flesh. Especially one of them, whom they called Kitty. The other one did not have a name yet. Probably Kitty was older. The Italian man thought and thought until he finally thought of a friend of his, a butcher who would give him a good price for Kitty. When he finished thinking, he rubbed his hands in satisfaction at the good business he would do with the goat.

* * *

Although it was already late in the fall, the days were still light and sunny, but a trifle cooler. One morning, Mereleh was awakened by a heart-rending scream. She felt like sleeping a bit later because it was Saturday and she did not have to go to school, but the scream upset her. It could only be the cry of a mother bereaved.

She looked out the window. The mama-goat, standing near the fence, lifted her head, shook her beard, looked this way and that, and screamed meh-meh, where are you, where are you. Then she stopped her screaming and began to whimper. Then Kitty's sister started crying her quivering meh-eh-eh. She, too, was now tied to a pole by a rope. She could not run to look for her sister. Then they both started over again. As the mama-goat finished her mournful wail the little goat would whimper her meh-eh-eh . . . where is my sister?

For several days they cried this way, from early morning to late at night. In the middle of the night you could hear the lonely, wretched cry of the goats. It kept everyone awake. It tore at everyone's heart. The neighbors were ashamed to show their faces at the windows. Each one of them felt some guilt in the disappearance of the little goat. Mereleh's father, who usually worked at home over his letters and papers, was unable to work. He could not find a place for himself. He would hold his head in his hands and groan. The weeping and the screams of the mama-goat and the sister-goat kept all the neighbors from calmly going about their daily chores.

On the evening of the fourth day the mama-goat was exhausted from her grieving. She lay down slowly on the grass, spent, her sides heaving and her eyes looking pitifully up at everyone passing by. The surviving little goat stood nearby and looked about her with frightened eyes.

And Mereleh stood at her window. She had asked her mother where Kitty had gone. But Mama had not answered her. Mama had made a nice soup for supper, with fresh, tasty meat, but Mereleh, because her mother had not answered her question, refused to come to the table. She stood alone at the window. She wanted to pour out her heart to someone. But neither her mother nor her father said a word. If only she had a sister . . .

But Mereleh did not have a sister. So she stood alone at
the window and stared into the evening blueness. And out
in the blueness, stood the little goat, staring back at her, staring, staring . . .

JONAH ROSENFELD

JONAH ROSENFELD

1882-1944

In the introduction to his six-volume collected works, (1924), Jonah Rosenfeld says: "The first things I wrote were pictures of ordinary life. Later I began to work my way into more involved themes and situations, and I worked my way in so far that I couldn't work my way out again . . ."

This is a characteristic of many of Jonah Rosenfeld's stories — psychological probing into the souls of his characters, finding the contradictory in the apparently harmonious, the extraordinary in the seemingly mundane, the pathetic in the comic.

Jonah Rosenfeld worked as a woodturner in Odessa for ten years—from the age of 13 to 23—and then decided to devote himself completely to writing. His first story, *"The Apprentice,"* published in 1904, was a portrayal of the life of a Jewish boy learning the woodturning trade. It was I. L. Peretz who, as he did with so many other young Jewish writers, read Jonah Rosenfeld's first work and encouraged him to continue. Delighted with the story, Peretz advised him to write about the life he knew best "from the inside."

Rosenfeld came to the United States in 1921 and joined the staff of the FORVERTS, where he stayed until his death. (It is known, however, that during the last years of his life, because of differences with the editor, Abe Cahan, some of his stories remained unpublished.)

Rosenfeld's stories are usually introspective, marked by an absorption with the wheels inside us, rather than with external events. His central figure is most often a confused individual in modern society, sitting in judgment upon himself. Even his own autobiography, *Eyner Aleyn,* (All Alone), is an example of this. While telling the not unusual story of a Jewish apprentice-boy, he probes the minds of the participants, including the author's.

Vreplamrendn

by Jonah Rosenfeld

WHAT THE WORD MEANS? It is not a word. It is not a word and it is not a name. I invented it myself. It came into my mind when—when the story I am about to tell took place . . . Took place? Actually, nothing very much took place. The essential thing here is that word. If it weren't for that word, there wouldn't be anything to tell. I said I invented the word myself. However, it's quite possible that among the "seventy languages" in the world, a word like that may be lying around loose somewhere. And who knows what such a word might mean in one of those languages? So I beg your pardon, I am hardly a linguist . . .

This was, yes—the first week I came here, to your country of stone and iron. I remember how the ground rocked under my feet, as though I were still on the ocean.

But before I get to the main plot, I'll give you a bit of my biography, so you can understand me better.

I came here with a few hundred dollars in my pocket. In general, my coming here was unnecessary. That is, not my coming here was unnecessary, but the whole idea itself. With the money I brought with me, and with the money I spent on the trip, and with the money I left behind with my wife and child, I could have made a nice living back in the old country. But I couldn't come to terms with my brother over the inheritance left us by my recently deceased father, so I relinquished my share. And then, finding the idea too painful that my brother should be left with the entire inheritance, I went off to America.

Just in passing, I must tell you also that I arrived here with a complete English vocabulary. That is, not that I knew English so well; it was the dictionary which I carried with me that knew English well. But not I. As soon as I stepped on board that ship I realized that no one understood a word of my English, and that I didn't understand a word of anybody else's. And this hurt me. It hurt me very much that when I asked the waiter for water he brought me butter.

I ask you to imagine the situation of an intelligent man who finds himself in a strange country where the language is not familiar to him. While I was *en route,* and during the few days I spent in hotels, I felt—well, not too bad. In a good many places, people are accustomed to foreigners. And aboard ship, who is a foreigner anyway? It's not a country. It's not a state. It's a place that hovers between heaven and earth, where every individual is thinking only about the journey, and where other people don't concern him, least of all the language they speak. National chauvinism is expunged from everyone.

No, I did not feel lonely then. I began to feel it only when I rented this room. Here, where I made my first home, I

began to feel it. And not particularly as a Jew, but simply as a foreigner who has wandered into a strange land.

My *lantsleit* and friends? That was precisely what I did *not* want. I didn't want them to know I was here. My wife's family were all here. But I didn't want any of them to know that I had come.

Ach, that journey to America! I have been here now for nine years, and I want you to know that back in those days, emigrating to America was an ordinary thing. I mean it was a thing for ordinary people. Whoever wasn't making a living in the old country—a workingman with a strong back and nothing to use it for—such people came to America. A tailor, a shoemaker who had chopped off his *"payess"* higher than his ears—such people came flying to America. But people of *our* kind stayed home. Times were better, times were worse—but we didn't think constantly about moving to America.

That's why I didn't want any of my *lantsleit* to know I was here. I didn't want them to gloat over me and feel more important than me with their knowledge of English (I can just imagine!) and their familiarity with the streets. I just didn't want that. I preferred to live here a little while, find some means of livelihood, get over my "greenness," and then—then, well, I would show up. I would show up and I would say to them—well, I wouldn't say anything, but the very fact that I would show up this way would say it for me: See! Who needs you anyway? I came here alone, I worked my way up alone, without coming to you or anyone else. I am I! At home I was I, and here, too, I am—I!

But in the meantime, I was lonely. And looking out the window at all the people passing by, I would think—there goes so-and-so, maybe a *lantsman* whom I don't recognize. It's silly to think they might have changed so much. I never thought, at the time, that I could have changed, too. So I stood at the window in my poor pedigreed loneliness, hoping that someone would recognize *me,* but I recognized no one and no one recognized me.

I also thought about a certain person . . . a girl . . . who, thanks to me, had run away to America. Perhaps, I thought, she too had passed before my window? Maybe she's one of those stout ladies there? Maybe she was sitting inside that big black shiny automobile that just flew by?

Just for instance, suppose she saw me, and recognized me, and was overjoyed to see me, and took me along with her . . . Understand? Practically my first day in the new country and I'm already flying away with a rich lady in a big car! Yes, I *am* a man with an extraordinary imagination. I have only to imagine a situation and I experience it with my emotions. And in my excitement I began to pace quickly back and forth across the length and breadth of my room. I don't remember, and I don't think I knew then either, how long I paced this way, but I was stopped by a knocking at my door.

"Come in!"

My door moved, opened, divided in two, one half to one side, the other half to the other side; and on the threshold between both doors, in all her massiveness, stood my landlady. With her thick white arms, bare up to her elbows, pushing open the big doors, she stood studying me with a reproachful smile on her face and said something in English. I recognized from her general expression that a declaration of love it was *not.* The truth is that she was not an unsympathetic woman, but full of charm and traces of a beauty that was hers in her youth—a beautiful head of hair, eyes and lips still youthful, with plenty of life and sparkle.

But I didn't know what had brought her here all of a sudden or what she wanted. She knew that I had just arrived from Europe and she knew that I did not understand English and yet she spoke to me in that language. Which showed that she must be very angry with me for something.

"Excuse me, missus," I said in Yiddish, "I don't understand what you're saying to me!"

Then she came out with *her* Yiddish. "This is not Europe, mister! In Europe everybody has a habit of pacing around the room and banging on floors. Here in America it's not the style. Here in America, if you want to take a walk, you go outside!"

Having said that, having given me a whole lecture about my European ungentlemanliness, apparently it wasn't enough for her, because she added something else in English at the end. Naturally, it must have been something worse than she had said in Yiddish, otherwise she would have finished in Yiddish. So I felt insulted and resentful, and I cried out: "Vreplamrendn!"

The word occurred to me on the spot and I said it with the sole purpose of telling her something she would not understand. And it worked. Furious, she exclaimed: "What!"

"Vreplamrendn, madam! Vreplamrendn!"

"What do you mean by *that*, Mister?" And she stood there for a moment with her arms spread out, leaning on both halves of the open door like one crucified. Her eyes flared with such dislike for me that my sides almost burst with the laughter exploding inside me, and I repeated the word so I wouldn't forget it, in order to have it ready for similar situations.

Finally, closing both doors and stepping out into the corridor, she said to herself, but to me, too: "Greenhorn!"

Then I opened the door hastily and called after her:

"Vreplamrendn, madam!"

MOISHE NADIR

182

MOISHE NADIR

1885-1943

The art of Moishe Nadir, who came to America when he was only 13, and who was writing in 1900, still has an ultra-modern ring. Critics have called him the greatest Jewish humorist since Sholem Aleichem, although his work is in a totally different style. In verse and short prose pieces he poked fun at the current scene in swift slashes, inventing new words, creating combinations of new and old words, making Yiddishisms out of Americanisms, in short, enriching the language in a unique style very difficult to imitate and often impossible to translate.

"Others write clever things for foolish people; I write foolish things for clever people," he said once. Quick to see the absurd in life, he especially delighted in deflating pomposity and "phoniness" wherever he discovered it—among friends or enemies. Nor did he spare his fellow critics, who, as he wrote in the foreword to his last book, "would never be able to forgive me for making light of their craft."

Nadir loved to perplex his readers with paradoxes, contradictions, absurdities, and he did it with a brilliance that can only be described as genius. Truly, nothing was sacred to him, not even his own importance in the general scheme of things. (Except perhaps for Narayev, his home town, which he knew only as a child.)

In his book *Nadirgang* (The Way of Nadir), published in 1937, he talks to his boyhood self of 37 years ago. "I can report to you now that the journey was not a 'success' . . . And although I can look you straight in the eye even today and say that 'you were a brave fellow,' nevertheless, beating your head against a wall—when the wall is made up of living human beings too—has come to naught . . . You tilted with the windmills that ground your bread—and ruined the windmill's wings along with your poor piece of bread, too!"

Although much of what Moishe Nadir wrote was topical, and many of his allusions and inventions intelligible only to the initiated, there is a great deal that still remains relevant—and funny.

The Eatabananists

by Moishe Nadir

*(A made-up tale without a word of
truth in it)*

OMEBODY TALKED ME into buying stock in a copper company. Stock and I are apparently not very close friends. You could even say—not friends at all. But since it was a matter of making a fortune (as the broker convinced me) I took my few hundred dollars, put them into stock, and waited for the moment when a special messenger would arrive with the news:

"I have the honor to report that you are finally a millionaire, *danke schön!*"

So I waited. Patiently waited. Hopefully waited. At any moment the stock would rise and I would become one of the big millionaires—please excuse the expression.

That stock of mine paid a dividend of 10 percent and cost 500 dollars a share. I bought five shares for 2500 dollars.

That was all the money I had, otherwise I would have bought more. Because who could stop me from making millions in such a fine, honest, tidy way? Who?

But remarkably—or to put it better—quite naturally, as soon as I bought my stock it began to drop, to sink, and it continued to drop and sink day after day. The dropping of my stock was so fast and so deep that it was barely visible to the naked eye. Whether it was raining outside, or whether the sun was shining brightly—my stock went its own way. It dropped . . .

Finally I said to my broker: "Mister, what will be the end of this dropping that my stock is dropping?"

He answered me coolly, as he flicked the ash off his expensive cigar with his little finger. "The present situation is quite natural. It's all because of . . . Brazil."

And he explained to me that because the Brazilian situation was now a difficult one and the banana crop there was a failure, this was reflected in the copper industry, and consequently also on our shares.

"Which means therefore," I said to myself, "that my whole destiny is now dependent on Brazil and its bananas. Good. I will hereafter keep an eye on Brazil and see what I can do to improve the situation of her bananas!"

So I thought. But my stock went its own way. It dropped. It dropped at a most astonishing speed. First 5 points, then 6, then 7, and so forth, until finally it was 35 percent lower than when I had bought it.

I began to hang around the pushcart peddlers. I asked them whether they bought bananas and how many, and did they buy those Brazilian fellows with the spotted bellies, like lizards. The peddlers looked at me very sympathetically and mostly replied that business was lousy and that as far as Brazil and her bananas were concerned, she could burn up like a match.

"Why?"

"Just so. No reason at all!"

As soon as I heard that, I ran all the way to my broker's and said: "Brazil should burn up like a match! Sell my stock and let there be an end to it!"

But the broker said: "You know what I'll tell you? This is just the right moment to buy more stock. Take my advice and buy another three-four shares and you'll soon be rich."

"Yes? How did you figure *that* out?"

"I figure," he said, "that with bananas, either the crop is good or it's poor. If it's poor, then we have bad bananas and the stock falls. But if they turn out to be good—"

"Then the stock drops anyway!" I finished for him.

"Wisecracks aside. Put a few more thousand into it. What can you lose?"

I called him a certain name and got out of there.

And my stock went its own way. It dropped. In the space of a few months it dropped 50 percent and meanwhile I concerned myself more and more with Brazil and her bananas. The devil! What kind of a miserly government was this Brazil? And why was she always in such a depressed condition?

So I thought. But I wasn't satisfied with merely thinking. I decided that direct action was needed to help the situation of my Brazilian brothers and through them the feeble condition of my stock, which had now dropped to a new low.

To this end I organized a society called "The Bananaphiles". The purpose of this society was to see that every member should eat as many bananas as possible, and if possible, a little more.

A noble purpose!

In the course of a few weeks, the Bananaphiles met several times in a cellar where bananas are ripened. There we stuffed ourselves full of these fat fruits. And when we began to feel bad, we started to agitate for setting up a nationwide movement in support of bananaphilism. Needless to say, or maybe it isn't needless, we were all shareholders in the same company.

Another month passed. Our bananaphiles meanwhile were raising a furor in the newspapers. Why weren't people eating more bananas? Why weren't the sick people in the hospitals given bananas to eat instead of questionable eggs and so forth?

The movement, with all the publicity in the press, took on gigantic di-men-zionen, as they say in German. "Eatabanana!" became a slogan, a signal, a password among lodgebrothers. The Eatabanana movement spread like a forest fire and captured the whole country. In all the vaudeville houses they sang Eatabanana! All the victrolas played it and famous dancers like la Duncan danced it in their barefeet, in several acts . . . The most important people in the country became Eatabananists or Bananaphiles. The finest ladies in the country did not stir out of their mansions without a basket of bananas under their arm.

In short, our tiny movement brought great fruits. The trade in bananas increased sharply, acquired a more dignified image. But on our stock—no effect whatsoever! The stock dropped. Again I ran to my broker's.

"Well? When will there be an end to the dropping that my stock is dropping? *Gevald!* I'm going broke, I am!" And I banged on the table with my fist, like this . . .

"*Sha!*" he said calmly. "What are you hollering about? Thank God, Brazil is allright!"

"The hell with Brazil!" I said. "What good is Brazil to me when I'm going broke? And besides, didn't you say that the reason my shares are in such bad shape is that Brazilian bananas aren't selling here? But what can you say now? Now—at a time when the whole country is caught up in the Eatabanana movement? Ha? How will you explain now why my shares are still dropping?"

"Well," he said, "it really *is* hard to explain. But if I were you, I'd buy a couple thousand dollars more of the same stock. Just for speculation. Because as soon as those shares stop falling, it's almost certain that they will either stay where they are, or they'll jump up so high you'll make money faster than you can count it—"

The end was that I barely dumped my shares at 60 percent loss, not counting trouble and heartache. And the only thing I got out of that stock was a ruined stomach from eating too many of those damned bananas . . .

Thoughts About Forty Cents

by Moishe Nadir

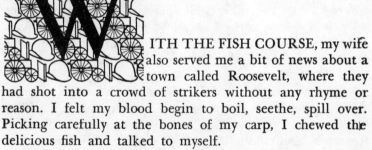

ITH THE FISH COURSE, my wife also served me a bit of news about a town called Roosevelt, where they had shot into a crowd of strikers without any rhyme or reason. I felt my blood begin to boil, seethe, spill over. Picking carefully at the bones of my carp, I chewed the delicious fish and talked to myself.

"Those vile capitalists! We ought to twist their heads off! Such swinish cannibals! Such cannibalistic swine!"

When my wife handed me the plate of soup, and I saw amidst the noodles the kind of marrow bone I love to chew on, my wrath cooled down somewhat, and blowing on the tasty soup I murmured to myself:

"Who knows, after all, which side is guilty? It's impossible that they would just go and shoot innocent people for nothing. For instance—has anyone shot at *you* lately?" (I said to myself.)

This logical argument pleased me immensely and I considered myself a thoughtful individual, a wise man, a radical thinker, and so on.

When my wife brought the meat to the table and I saw the two chicken wings and a sweet chicken-liver and a splendid chicken-leg—I began to see the situation in a completely new light. Munching on the white wing and washing it down with a glass of good wine, I began to see that the whole thing was not so terrible as it had appeared during the fish course, and that you have to give the other side a chance to tell its story, too.

"Who knows!" I asked myself as I chewed on the chicken leg. "Who knows whether those strikers aren't really dangerous? And why (I thought further) should poor people strike anyway? Who asked them to? If the Law (I said) *ordered* them to strike, well, that would be a different story. But as long as the Law allows you to live on a dollar-and-sixty-cents a day, and doesn't bother you—then why should you go out and strike for a lousy 40 pennies a day? Really! It's ridiculous!"

When my wife brought me the wonderful apple compote and a piece of fresh strudel, I took another look at the piece of news about the shooting of the strikers in the town of Roosevelt, and sipping the last of my Turkish demitasse, I said to myself (and I could feel my blood starting to boil again):

"What the hell is the matter with those strikers, anyway! What are they making such a fuss about! They must have exactly $2 a day? In the first place, how do they know the bosses can afford $2 a day? Maybe they don't have it. Maybe they don't want to. Maybe they don't have any time to bother with the whole thing.

"And in the second place, if they *do* go out on strike—why *not* shoot them? If (I said to myself as I cleaned my teeth with a toothpick) if in Europe they are shooting thousands of people who are *not* striking, then why shouldn't we here be allowed to shoot a couple dozen foolish workers who are striking for a lousy 40 cents a day? It's ridiculous, that's what it is!"

And only at this point, (when I lit up my fine Havana cigar and made myself comfortable on my soft easy-chair), did I see with brilliant clarity how silly, how trivial those workers are. For a measly 40 cents a day, to make all that commotion and even risk their necks!

I couldn't help laughing, really I couldn't . . .

The Power of A Bull

by MOISHE NADIR

NE MORNING I LOOKED OUT my window and there, on an empty lot across the street, they had put up a billboard. And on the billboard was a new sign—so fresh that the paste was still wrinkling the edges—BULL FORUM TOBACCO! THE BEST AND MOST AROMATIC TOBACCO IN THE WHOLE WORLD! WHY NOT SMOKE BULL FORUM! ONLY 10c a PACK! SMOKE BULL FORUM AND BE STRONG AS A BULL! (Here there was a picture of a bull.)

As I read this sign I began to feel a sort of uneasiness, a feeling that this bullish announcement was going to cause me trouble, although I'm not even a smoker, generally speaking. (I smoke only when someone offers me a cigarette.)

On my way to work that morning, as I passed the billboard, I again heard with my eyes the wild cry of the
printed Bull, telling me that there was nothing better in
the whole world than BULL FORUM tobacco and that I
must buy a pack for 10c.

"Not now, please," I implored, "not now. I have to go to
work. Some other time, maybe. Right now I don't have
the time . . ."

"But it's only 10c a pack!" the sign screamed at my back.

"It's not the money!" I argued without turning around.
"Ten cents means nothing to me. It's only that I'm not a
smoker—on my honor!"

"But it's the best tobacco in the world!" the Bull boomed.

"It's even better than that!" I agreed, apologetically. "But
what can I do if I don't smoke!"

I walked away as rapidly as I could, but I felt the Bull
panting after me, about to impale me on his horns because
I refused to buy a pack of his tobacco—at least one pack
for 10c.

When I came into the shop I was pale as a corpse. All day
I imagined the wild Bull standing behind me with his cap
to one side, his coat unbuttoned, his beard unkempt, demanding that I tell him why I refused to buy a pack of
BULL FORUM. It didn't take long, however, before I
realized that the Bull with the cap on the side was not really
a bull but my foreman, demanding angrily of me why
my work was going so slowly today.

How could I tell him!

On my way home I again had to pass the BULL FORUM
sign. When I came close enough I said:

"On my honor, I don't smoke, really. I don't believe in it."

"What do you mean, you don't believe in it! 80 million
people believe in it—and *you* don't? Only 10c a pack—the
most aromatic tobacco in the world! Everybody smokes

BULL FORUM!"

Wherever I went the words rang in my ears and danced before my eyes—at home, in the shop, in the street, in my dreams. . . .

And after three weeks, when my Bull had grown older and dirtier and swollen from the rain, he looked even fiercer than before. And after a storm ripped off one of his horns he became so bitterly angry that his BULL FORUM TO-BACCO (in giant letters) sounded like a final warning, an ultimatum. Every morning, we—I and the Bull and the sign —had the following conversation:

"Well, have you bought a pack of BULL FORUM or not? Gr-r-r-."

"I will, I will. Stop growling—"

"When will you buy it? Gr-r-r—" (He prepares to spring at me.)

(I fall back.) "Don't! I'm going over to the cigar-store right now and buy a pack!"

"Remember! Gr-r-r—"

That evening, as I passed the sign on my way home, I took out my pack of BULL FORUM (which I had bought) and waved it at him. But he did not stop his bellowing:

"BUY BULL FORUM TOBACCO!"

"I did! I already bought some! See!"

"BUY BULL FORUM TOBACCO!"

"I'm telling you, I did! Look! Here it is!"

But he kept on bellowing. BUY BULL FORUM TO-BACCO!

At this point I lost my temper. I counterattacked. I tore the Bull off the billboard. I screamed like a man demented.

"Buy BULL FORUM—hah! Take that! The best tobacco—
. hah! Take that! Ten cents a pack—hah! Take that! I ripped him to shreds with my bare hands. . . .

Twenty minutes later I was in jail for destroying private property.

A *Few Observations*

NOT EVERYTHING is gold that doesn't glitter.
Not everything which lacks lustre is real art.

Not all who boast that they can't write are great writers. A person may not know any grammar, he may construct bad sentences, he may be careless of punctuation—and still be a botcher.

And contrariwise: A man may have an outstanding style, he may write clearly and to the point, and still be a good writer.

Not everything that wraps itself in fog is art; not everything that grates on the ear is music; and not everyone with dirty fingernails is a Maxwell Bodenheim.

———

A REAL-LIFE apple does not have to try to look like an apple. It's not even so terrible if it looks like something else. A real-life apple—even if it doesn't have the seal of a Notary Public that it's an apple—people believe it anyway.

But a rubber apple must be as thoroughly apple-ish as possible. A rubber apple can under no circumstances permit itself to be as non-apple-ish as a real-life apple sometimes is. Therefore we demand of imitative artists and writers that their people must be as natural as possible.

Contrariwise, in Dostoevski, a human being may sometimes look like a cube of sugar with two eyes—and it doesn't matter. Because the human being *is alive*.

THE MARVELS of civilization:

For a mere 10c you can sit down in a cool hall with a lot of ventilation and music, and while you sit there in the coolness, and the electric fans fan you, you watch on a screen how human beings are torn apart by grenades; you see trains sliding off rails and airplanes crashing; you see men dying in coal mines under the earth and ships sinking into the depths of the waters; you see little children burned to death and run over by trucks.

All these interesting calamities you see for only 20c—10c for you and 10c for your wife—and you comment to her how nice and cool it is and would she like a piece of chocolate. Or maybe a glass of soda water. And tomorrow, if we live, let's go to the beach. . . .

PAPA, WHY is it raining today from heaven? Why don't they fix the sky up there, so it doesn't leak?

The sky leaks, my child, because it is broken. Because the human prayers and cries which reach to heaven tear the blue lining. Because the blond Angel who rides on the moon-crescent sticks out his feet and makes holes in the sky. Because God Himself often loses His patience and grabs a piece of sky and tosses it over his shoulder like an opera-singer—He wants to run away somewhere, but doesn't have any place to run to. Because the millions of longing eyes which look up to Heaven rub holes in the delicate texture.

That's why it rains so much, my child.

Lazer-Elya's 3 Patents
Against War (1916)

1.

IT'S A SIMPLE PATENT. Which it won't cost a penny
and you won't have to make any revolutions or anything.
Well, go ahead and explain it.

My patent is that the soldiers of both sides should exchange their uniforms. You catch on, Mr. Nadir?

Not exactly.

For instance: the German soldiers should exchange with
the French soldiers, and put on each other's uniforms.

So what will happen?

What's so hard to understand? When the Germans see
the Frenchmen in German uniforms, they'll think they are
Germans, and they won't shoot. The same with the French
and all the others. In that way, the wars will be abolished.
You like that patent?

Well, in-and-of-itself the patent is all right. But you forgot
one thing, Lazer-Elya. When the German exchanges his uni-
form for a French one, he will be dressed in French clothes,
right? So, when he looks at himself in the mirror he'll think
he's a Frenchman, and he'll shoot himself as his own enemy.
That's something you forgot completely, Lazer-Elya.

(Lazer-Elya bows his head and thinks a while, but not for
long.)

Wait a minute, Mr. Nadir! I have another patent for that.
In order to prevent the soldiers from shooting themselves,

we'll make a rule that before a soldier goes out on the bat-
tlefield, his hands must be tied behind him!

2

I have a patent against the submarines, too.

For instance?

Very simple. The submarines go under the ocean, right?

Right.

If it wasn't for the ocean the submarines would be kaput,
right?

Right.

That being the case, I have a patent—listen and pay attention. Make a hole in the bottom of the ocean and let out
all the water. That's all there is to it!

3.

This is the best patent of them all, Mr. Nadir. Why should
we shoot bullets and shrapnel and all the other things and
make wounds which they have to be bandaged up with
cotton? Better let's shoot the cotton in the first place and be
done with it! Write about that to President Wilson. I'm sure
he'll like my suggestion!

CHAVER PAVER

202

CHAVER PAVER

Gershon Einbinder

1900-1965

"As a boy I loved to make up stories and tell them to my friends . . . Naturally, not all the stories were completely my own; I took many of them from the legends I used to hear Jews telling each other in the old synagogue, at dusk, behind the stove . . .

"My very first *written* story was in Hebrew, and it didn't end happily—for me. I was about 12, and I was attending Yankl Lipman's *cheder*. I wrote this story about a baby goat who didn't like the idea of his mother being milked every morning before he had had his breakfast, so he protested to the townspeople, who grew very angry and sold the baby goat to the butcher. Yankl Lipman read my story and laughed, then he read it to the boys in the cheder and they laughed, too. But they were making fun of me, and after that I didn't write another thing for years. Not until the time of the revolution and the pogroms . . .

"In Kishinev, I became a teacher in a school for refugees. I had always loved to tell stories to children . . . so I wrote down my first Yiddish story and the children in the kindergarten loved it. And that was when I took the name Chaver Paver. I thought: anybody who writes for children should have a playful name, one that will itself make the children smile. I remembered a ditty I used to sing as a child which started with those two words—*chaver paver*—so that became my pen-name.

"When I came to America (in 1923) I continued writing for children. But at a summer camp once, I suddenly felt the urge to write something about Brownsville . . .

"Why does one write? To tell a story, so that it may remove us for a little while from the sadness and the drabness of life. And if the story itself must describe this sadness, this drabness, then one can always add other colors to bring out the festive and joyous side of life too . . ."

(Excerpted from an interview with Chaver Paver in *Yiddishe Kultur*, February 1961).

Gershon

by Chaver Paver

First Time on East Broadway

NOW FELL IN AMERICA. Gershon strolled along the whitened streets and forgot he was in the new country.

The snow made the alien streets familiar and homey. He walked to Sutter Avenue Station. There he would put a nickel into a slot and the gate would open and let him through. He would run up the stairs to the platform high above the street. A train would come from the direction of Canarsie, and with its six or seven cars it would look like a serpent, a giant serpent. The train would stop, the doors would spring open and he would enter a car with straw benches. He would take a seat near the window and look out; the entire trip he would look out the window.

The train would race high above the streets of Brooklyn, its roofs, its houses. He would ride across the city and come to a tremendous bridge, the Williamsburg Bridge, which hangs in mid-air on a million wires, and the wires would look like the strings of a harp beckoning to be played. And when the train would be riding along this tremendous bridge he would see in the distance another tremendous bridge, also hanging in the air—the Brooklyn Bridge. . . .

He would also see a river, which from that height looks like a thin strip of water, and in the river he would see barges and ships. He would see the skyscrapers on the other side of the bridge, with their thousands and thousands of windows. Then the train would slide underground and stop at Essex Street. On Essex Street, Gershon would race up the steps and head toward East Broadway and even before he reached East Broadway he would see the only big building in the neighborhood, a ten-story building with a Yiddish sign on the roof reading FORVERTS.

Gershon knew he would see all these things because his sister Rochel had described the entire route to him in every detail. He was bringing a story to the FORVERTS, a story he had written in the evening after work. Four weeks it had taken him to write it. It was about his sister Rochel and her life in America, and he had called it "The Lucky Girl."

His job in a ladies' garment shop as a cutter was not going so well. Poor Rochel, who worked in the same place, had to suffer shame and embarrassment on his account. The scissors refused to obey Gershon's fingers, they refused to follow the white chalk-line marked on the cloth. Yet Gershon had such long and nimble fingers. Why did they lose their suppleness when they picked up a scissors?

And to make matters worse, the people in the shop learned that Gershon was a writer. That was all they needed. It was his sister who had first announced proudly that her brother was a writer. Afterwards she was sorry, because everybody made fun of him. And the boss, after four weeks, realizing that Gershon would never make a "mechanic," fired him with these words: "As a cutter you seem to be a very good writer. . . ."

And his *lantsleit* advised him that if he could get something into the FORVERTS he would be "allright."

So here was Gershon on Essex Street, on Delancey, and then on Broome and Grand, and everywhere "our brothers, the sons of Israel." They made the streets and the whole neighborhood lively, with their lively eyes, their lively gestures, their lively voices. Not only the peddlers at their pushcarts, but even the ordinary passers-by. They walked along with such animated bodies, with such tremendous vivacity, with such a tremendous passion for life. They stepped quickly, the men in black derbies, wrapped in coats and sweaters; the women in knitted woolen hats, also wrapped in coats and sweaters. They stepped quickly in the white, shiny winter's day and a blue-white steam puffed from their mouths as though they were all smoking cigarettes.

About this Jewish East Side and its tenement houses Gershon had read even while he was still in Roumania. And according to the books, life was all gloom and wretchedness on the Jewish East Side of New York. Well, the dirty, peeling walls of the tenements against the whiteness of the snow were indeed gloomy and wretched. But the people rushing along the streets—what an air of confident faith, of strength, of lust for life they had!

And here was Gershon standing before the high, lofty FORVERTS building. He noticed that nearby were also the offices of the TOG, another Yiddish newspaper, but they were in a small, narrow building, with three or four stories, and alongside the haughty, craning ten stories of the FORVERTS building they seemed puny and pitiful.

One gets up to the ninth floor, where the editorial offices are, in something called an "elevator." And the elevator-man

inspected Gershon with mockery in his eyes. He was a Jew
in a grey cap, the peak a little to one side; his back was a
little bent, his eyes a little bulgy, and his mouth wide and
a little sneering. Even his rasping voice was a little mocking as he said to Gershon:

"*A shreiberl?*"

Gershon said nothing. He kept his eyes averted as he
waited impatiently for the elevator to reach the ninth floor.
The corridor was clean and tidy. And the big office he entered breathed with a pleasant, friendly warmth. He could
see at once that this was an editorial office. Writers sat at
tables immersed in their work. Several doors bore the names
of well-known writers, familiar to him from the columns of
the FORVERTS.

"Who are you looking for?" asked an older man with a
sharp and inquisitive face. A pair of slightly crossed eyes
looked out at Gershon through a pince-nez with gold frames.

"I would like to see the editor, Abe Cahan."

"I'm Abe Cahan," said the man very cordially.

"I've brought a story," Gershon said simply. He had not
expected such good fortune. Abe Cahan took the manu-
script from him and read it right on the spot. Or rather, he
ushered Gershon into his own office, asked him politely to
sit down, and then read the story through carefully. Eventually he said:

"This is no good for the FORVERTS."

Gershon did not even ask why. He found his way back to
the corridor. He could not bear to face the elevator-man with
the mocking sneer. He made his way down the stairs. There
must have been three hundred of them. . . .

A *Temporary Job*

JUST BEFORE the High Holy Days, David Ignatov found Gershon a little job where he could earn a few dollars. He sent him out to put up HIAS posters in the synagogues all over Greater New York. These posters called upon the Jews to contribute generously to HIAS, the organization which was such a big help to the Jewish immigrants all over the world. The posters were printed in colors and showed an old Jewish man with a sack over his shoulder and a staff in his hand, gazing helplessly at the stormy waters of the sea.

It was hard work. Gershon had to carry a big pack of posters on the subways from place to place (wherever there was a synagogue), tack them up, and then come back for more.

And where were the Jewish synagogues of New York to be found? Where were they *not* to be found? On the East Side and on the West Side, in Harlem and in the Bronx, in Williamsburg and in Brownsville, in Brighton and in Coney Island. Everywhere. Jews had come to New York, and before they were in the new country two months they had managed in one way or another to set up a *shul*.

For Gershon it was a cultural-historical expedition. He was intrigued by the names of the synagogues. Many of them bore the names of towns in Ukrainia, Poland, Roumania. "*Beyss-HaKnesset* Such-and-Such-a-Town." An inscription like this on a synagogue moved Gershon deeply. There was a great deal of emotional association in such a name for Jews who came from that town. The newly-arrived immigrants needed to comfort each other in the new country, to be together in their hours of worship, to speak with each other as they had done "at home," with all the idioms and localisms and speech-tones.

That was at the beginning, years and years ago. Then the members of the "Congregation Such-and-Such-a-Town" dispersed to the ends of New York and other Jews worshipped in the synagogue with the old name. Maybe on Rosh Hashonah or Yom Kippur *lantsleit* came from distant neighborhoods to pray in their old synagogues, or maybe on an ordinary day a man would get homesick and come downtown to *davn*. Here and there you might even find one or two of the "ancients" who had not moved away. . . .

Apparently, in the early years when Jews began to come to America, most of the little synagogues were such *"Anshei Bnai"* congregations. Later, when the Jews spread out all over New York, the larger synagogues were established which gave themselves generalized, symbolic names—*Aytz Chaim* (Tree of Life), *Shaarei Tfila* (Gates of Prayer), *Shaarei Shomayim* (Gates of Heaven), and so on.

In these larger synagogues Gershon rarely found anyone sitting over a Talmud and studying. Most of them were closed on weekdays, and he usually had to go looking for the *shammos* to open the door so he could tack up the HIAS poster.

In the small synagogues his job was easy. They were always open; there was always someone inside either studying a sacred book or teaching children. In one such synagogue in the Bronx Gershon fell asleep, so tired was he from running around the Bronx with his posters. Outside the heat was unbearable, but inside the semidark synagogue it was cool and cozy. Outside, the urgent, clamorous American life roared and jangled; inside, a truly Holy Place, an ancient, humble Holy Place, where the voice of Torah never ceases. An old Jew with a long white beard swayed over a Talmud to the cadences of the age-old chant.

Gershon sat down in this synagogue to rest and was soon lost in the past. He saw himself swaying over a Talmudfolio in the days when he had been a Yeshiva student. Then he fell asleep and forgot completely about America. For fifteen or twenty minutes he slept this way, but it was a long, long time since his sleep had been so sweet. . . .

And when he awoke, he felt a deep longing. What the longing was for he did not know, but it gnawed and gnawed at him. . . .

Yom Kippur
In Brownsville

YOM KIPPUR morning no one in Brownsville went to work. Yom Kippur morning there was not a single home in Brownsville where an alarm clock was allowed to scream. Yom Kippur morning it was so quiet in Brownsville that Gershon couldn't sleep. It was even quieter than on Sunday mornings. Sunday mornings you might hear an occasional car or truck riding by. Yom Kippur morning—not a truck, not a car, as though the street had gone into hiding, afraid to utter a sound. Even on Kol Nidre night, cars were rare in Brownsville. The Brownsville taxis, which usually cruise on Pitkin Avenue, disappeared. Pitkin Avenue itself, where even on a *Shabbos* you could find stores and restaurants open, had been dark since the previous evening.

Gershon had gone to the Thatford Avenue Synagogue for Kol Nidre. He had felt homesick for the Kol Nidre evenings of Bershad, but when he entered the synagogue he grew even more so. Here in the Thatford Avenue *shul* there were also big candles burning on the Reader's Platform, and many of the men were dressed in white *Kittls*. Missing, however, was

Hirshke Redhead, the *chazzan* of the old synagogue in Ber-shad. When Hirshke Redhead used to begin Kol Nidre in his pious but powerful voice, the gates of heaven opened, and a sacred tremor went through the synagogue. Himself a complete pauper, Hirshke had had plenty of complaints to the Almighty, not only those of the congregation, but his own personal ones. . . .

Here in the Thatford Avenue Synagogue there was a famous cantor who demanded a big fee and who sang the Kol Nidre with his choir as though he were giving a concert. Missing here, too, was Gershon's father, tall in his white *kittl*, with his old heirloom *tallis* covering his head. On Kol Nidre night and all the next day of Yom Kippur his father rarely sat down; all day he stood on his feet, absorbed in his prayers and his thoughts.

But Gershon loved Brownsville on that clear, autumn Yom Kippur day as he strolled along the streets which the golden autumn sun had painted with magic colors. They were deserted, these Brownsville streets. The entire adult population was inside the synagogues. Only one man was not in shul—*Moishe der meshugener*. Dirty-faced, slovenly, he walked on Pitkin Avenue all alone with his sack of rags over his shoulder. Nor did he even stop to cry out, as was his practice: "May America burn up! I'd rather go to Phila-delphia!" What was the use of crying and complaining when there was not another living soul on the street to hear?

And there were so many synagogues in Brownsville—one for perhaps every two blocks. Of course, many of them were only temporary synagogues, in a store, or a private house, and after the holidays they would "adjourn" for another year. But there were also a great many permanent syna-gogues, and near one of these, on Herzl Street, Gershon saw signs of a commotion. A congregant in the women's section had fainted, probably from fasting, and they had brought her outside, and a doctor was immediately found among the worshippers, and with his *tallis* still on his shoulders he bent over her and felt her pulse. . . .

Gershon's mother, too, had been in the habit of fainting, almost every Yom Kippur. . . .

Gershon Pushes A Wheelbarrow

GERSHON HAD a hard time finding a job in America. Other greenhorns, for instance his *lantsman* Alter Windfeld, the slender, handsome fellow with the silken-black, beaming eyes who also lived in Brownsville, was a knitter in a sweater factory and made piles of money. Pressers in the dress trade, fur workers, painters, also made piles of money, and every greenhorn dreamed of learning one of these trades.

How does one get into such a trade? A relative, or a *lantsman,* or a good friend, takes you up to his shop and does everything he can to persuade the boss to give you a chance. But as far as Gershon was concerned, not one *lantsman* and not one good friend wanted to take him into his shop. They simply refused to believe that he, an educated young man and a writer in the bargain, would ever be able to learn a trade. Instead, they laughed at him whenever he pleaded with them to find him a job in a shop. "Go on, forget it! Don't be foolish, you'll never do for that kind of work!"

So Gershon, became a "common laborer"—that is, he did various kinds of heavy and unskilled work. At that time they were erecting on Sutter Avenue a big movie-house called "The Palace" and Gershon was hired to load and cart out the debris—sand, stones, bricks, lumber, and so forth.

The foreman was a German with dull-grey eyes in a lumpish face, and he took an instant dislike to Gershon. Maybe it happened because they could not communicate with each other too readily. Gershon knew no German, and, of course, no English. Or maybe it was because Gershon was physically the exact opposite of the foreman. That young man was a fellow with iron hands and broad bones. Gershon was thin and delicate. Or maybe it was simply because he hated Jews. Whatever it was, he didn't allow Gershon a moment's rest. The wheel-barrow was made of iron, with one wheel, and you had to be pretty strong to push it amidst the debris that lay around the building site. But Gershon had made up his mind, as though his very life depended on it, that he, the learner with the delicate hands, would master that heavy, obstinate wheelbarrow. But once in a while he needed to rest for a moment. No sooner would the thought enter his mind, however, than he heard the voice of the bully: "Come on! Get a move on!"

The foreman later learned to regret his actions, after he took a beating—not from Gershon—but from the Jewish painters who worked on the building. And the foreman never even knew who hit him, because the attack came from every direction. A smack in the back of the neck. He whirled around. A painter stood there innocently wielding his brush. Again a smack in the back of the neck. He whirled around. Nobody there but a painter hard at work on the wall. And there were eight painters on that job! Eventually he came to understand that the Jewish painters were taking the part of "one of their own" and he let Gershon alone.

So Gershon, after work, runs through the streets of Brownsville tired, exhausted, faint with hunger. (Whenever he is cold and hungry, he must keep moving quickly. In Odessa, as a boy, he also used to run through the streets when he was hungry.) But soon he'll feel better. Mrs. Siegal's kitchen is wonderfully warm, and from the big pots on her big iron stove come tantalizing aromas of pea-soup and *russel-fleysh*. And the table is set with big plates of sliced pumpernickel and little dishes of herring and tomatoes.

The tall, broad-beamed Mrs. Siegel feeds Gershon and his sister breakfasts and suppers for fifteen dollars a week. She loves to set out big, overflowing platters, and she is happiest when nothing is left over. So Gershon sees to it that nothing is ever left in those big plates, but he still stays hungry. And when he runs out on his way to night-school he never fails to stop into the candy store for a bar of chocolate.

On the darkening streets of Brownsville, thousands of people are again rushing to and fro, but this is a different kind of rushing than the early-morning rush to work. This is a joyful movement of young fellows and girls, immigrant fellows and girls who have been in the country two, three or at most six months. Dressed up in their new American clothes, bought for them by their relatives the first week they arrived, they now rush through the Brownsville streets on their way to the night-schools, spacious red-bricked buildings with large, brightly-lit windows.

In a warm, brightly-lit classroom, with a large blackboard covering the entire front wall, with world maps spread over the other walls, with the American flag standing in a corner, Gershon and other brand-new greenhorns sit at desks used by schoolchildren during the day, small desks, and Gershon doesn't know what to do with his long legs.

The teacher teaches the class the skill of spelling "night," which is almost like the Yiddish *"nacht"* but which has that extra "g" in the middle: "Sister," which means *"shvester,"* is a pleasure to spell, without any extra letters at all. But "knife," with that unnecessary "k" right smack at the beginning!

And the gang of greenhorns have all put in a hard day's work in the shop. You can see that in their tired fingers which hold the pens, But not in their eyes. Their eyes are all asparkle with the desire to learn, to know. . . .

Glossary

agada — The allegorical or story portion of the Talmud, as distinct from the legal portion.

alrightnik — (American Yiddishism) One who has achieved financial success. Often used derisively for one who, because of this success, behaves in an overbearing manner.

ARBEITER TSEITUNG — Yiddish newspaper of the Socialist-Labor Party; it was founded in 1890 and lasted for about five years.

ashrey yoshvey veysecho — Hebrew phrase which begins the *mincha,* the afternoon prayers. "Happy are they who dwell in Thy house."

beyss-haKnesset — A synagogue

Bund — Short form for *Algemeiner Yiddishn Arbeterbund.* (General Jewish Labor Federation), founded in 1897 to organize Jewish workers in Russia, Poland and Lithuania. A "bund" is an alliance.

chazzan — Cantor. Traditionally, the cantor was also supposed to be a man of some learning.

chevra — A congregation or society. Can also mean a gang, a band.

chosid — A disciple of one of the *chasidic* rabbis; a follower of the *chasidic* teachings. Also, an enthusiast, an ardent fan. Some of the famous Yiddish actors, for example, had their own *"chasidim."*

Daitch — A German. Also, a German Jew. Somewhat scornfully, a Jew who has become "Westernized."

ganef — A thief. Used also for a sly, clever fellow. The adjective *"ganeyvish"* connotes craftiness: *ganeyvishe shtik* — sly tricks.

gemora — that part of the Talmud which is the commentary on the original *mishna*. A *"gemora-kop"* is a keenly-discerning mind.

Gerer rebbe — The *chasidic* rebbe of Ger, the Polish town of Gura Kalvarya. The *Gerer Rebbe* was the leader of the most popular dynasty in Poland.

gevald! — literally, violence. A cry for help. *"Gevaldik"* also connotes immensity: *gevaldik groys* — tremendously big.

goy (pl. *goyim*) — literally, nation. It has come to mean all non-Jews. Also, a Jew who behaves in an "unJewish" manner. A Jew not versed in Jewish learning. In the judgment of the orthodox, a non-observant Jew.

grober yung — uncouth fellow, a boor, an ignoramus.

kaddish — The prayer recited in memory of the departed. Used in colloquial Yiddish to refer to a son, (who will say the *kaddish* on the death of the parent.)

kedusha — a responsive prayer in the *shemone esra* (the Eighteen Benedictions) led by the cantor or Reader.

kinnder — literally, children. Used also as an endearing term of address among friends.

kittl — white linen coat worn on solemn occasions.

k'n'hora — literally, "no evil eye." A formula for warding off evil spirits. Now used almost automatically by Yiddish speakers to denote admiration.

kneydlech — Dumplings, made of matzo meal, mainly a Pesach dish. *"Er meynt nit di hagada nor di kneydlech"* — he has in mind not so much the recital of the *Hagada* as the meal. That is, he is talking about spiritual things but really means the material.

kovid — literally, honor. Approval by one's associates or the community.

krishma — The recital of the *Shema* ("Hear O Israel, the Lord our God, the Lord is One.") Uttered thrice daily. Usually, however, this refers to the prayer recited before retiring.

lantsfroi — feminine of *lantsman*

lantsleit — plural of *lantsman*

lantsman — A man who hails from the same town as you in the old country. (From the word *"land,"* country)

lantsmanshaft — A society of *lantsleit*. The *lantsmanshaft* became an important form of organization among the immigrants.

liebinke — darling

mazel-tov — A wish for good luck. Congratulations!

medina — A country or state. "Columbus's *medina*" was used derisively for the United States.

melamed — a Hebrew-School teacher. A teacher in a *cheder*. Colloquially, also a naive, unworldly fellow.

mentsh — literally, a human being. Connotes a decent, compassionate person. It also means a hired hand, an employee.

meshuga, meshugener — Crazy; a crazy man. The word is used in Yiddish loosely, as it is in English.

mincha — The afternoon prayers, recited up to sunset.

minyan — A quorum for public worship: ten men above the

age of 13. Women are not counted as part of the "official" congregation.

mishna — The basic statement of the Law in the Talmud. The authors of the *mishna* were known as *tannaim* (teachers).

mitzva — literally, a commandment. It has also come to mean "a good deed," because the 613 codified commandments of Jewish life covered also the relationships between man and his fellows.

pickeven — (American Yiddishism)   to picket.

pesachdik — ritually kosher for Passover (*pesach*).

Rashi — Abbreviation for Rabbi Shlomeh Yitzchoki (1040-1105), who wrote commentaries on the Bible and Talmud. His work and his name have become synonymous.

Reb — Title before a name, "Mister."

rebbe—rabbi or teacher. Often, the leader of a *chasidic* dynasty.

russel-fleysh — pot roast.

seder — literally, order. The Passover service at home.

shabbos — The Sabbath day of rest. The Jewish Sabbath became a looked-for day of spiritual and physical refreshment.

shammos — Sexton of a synagogue. But the *shammos'* duties were (and still are) more varied. He also performs certain functions in the absence of the cantor. The *shammos* of the *chasidic rebbe* was rather like an adjutant.

shlimmazl — luckless one. Ill luck itself. Also, a clumsy person.

shmuess — A chat.

shreiberl — Shreiber is Yiddish for writer. The diminutive "l" here is a mark of disdain.

Shulchan Aruch — Literally, The Prepared Table. The code of laws which presents Jewish practices in a simplified and codified way. It became the ultimate authority for strict adherents to Jewish religious tradition.

skitze — A short sketch. (Literary term)

tachlis — Practical and purposeful activity. The opposite of aimlessness.

tallis — A prayer shawl. The fringes on the corners are the essential part of the prayer shawl, being a "reminder of the covenant between God and the Jews."

Tosefos — (pronounced toysfes) Notes on the Talmud. "Additions"

treyf — Ritually impure. Forbidden food. Also, something taboo, shady or unlawful . . .

tsatske — literally, a toy. Something you want to show off with. Used also in a negative sense.

tsimmes — Stewed fruit or vegetables. Dessert. Also, used ironically when too much importance is attached to unimportant things — *"machn a tsimmes"* — to make a whole *tsimmis* out of it.

Voskhod — (Sunrise) A Russian-language Jewish periodical published in Petersburg around the turn of the century.

yeshiva — An academy. A school of Jewish learning.

yeshiva bocher — A boy or young man who attends a *yeshiva*.

Yiddishkeit — Jewishness. Also, Judaism.

yortseit — Anniversary of a death. Observed by the lighting of a candle at home and the recital of the *kaddish* in the synagogue.

Yunge — *Di Yunge*, The Young Ones. A "school" of Yiddish poets in America who rebelled against the formalism and the "message verses" of their predecessors.

MAX ROSENFELD has been translating Yiddish poetry and prose for various periodicals for more than a decade. His work is represented in several anthologies of Jewish writing. Most recently, he co-edited and translated a volume of Morris Rosenfeld's selected poetry and prose. A native of Philadelphia, he is a teacher in a Jewish school and a writer and lecturer on Jewish cultural themes.

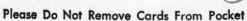